I obeyed her. T
manage. They were tight.
inches below the dark bands of the stocking tops. I would have difficulty in walking in them, I said. The corset nipped my waist. My hips blossomed. The corset framed my navel beneath an upward curve. My belly gleamed white.

"You will walk in them slowly and with stately tread—that is their purpose, Beatrice. Try."

I moved from her. I walked. The high heels teetered. My legs were constrained. I felt the movements of my bottom, naked . . .

Also available from Headline

Eros in the Country
Eros in Town
Eros on the Grand Tour
Venus in Paris
A Lady of Quality
Sweet Fanny
The Love Pagoda
The Education of a Maiden

Maid's Night In

Anonymous

HEADLINE

First published in Great Britain in 1989
by HEADLINE BOOK PUBLISHING PLC

ISBN 0 7472 3333 0

Printed and bound in Great Britain by
Collins, Glasgow

HEADLINE BOOK PUBLISHING PLC
Headline House
79 Great Titchfield Street
London W1P 7FN

Maid's Night In

ONE

I DO not like old rooms that are brown with the smell of time.

The ceilings in my husband's house were too high. They ran away from me. In the night I would reach up my hands but I could not touch them. When Edward asked me what I was doing I said I was reaching my hands up to touch the sky. He did not understand. Were we too young together?

Once a week he would remove my nightdress and make love to me. Sometimes I moved, sometimes I did not. Sometimes I spoke, sometimes I did not speak. I did not know the words to speak. We quarrelled. His stepmother would scold us. She could hear. In the large, high-ceilinged rooms voices carried as burnt paper flies, rising, tumbling, falling. Drifting.

The doors were always half open. Sometimes—lying in bed as if upon a huge cloud—I would play with his prick, his cock, his pintle. Pintle. I do not like the *nt* in it. Sometimes I would turn and he would rub it against the groove in my bottom. I liked that. I lay with my nightgown up, my back to him, and had my dreams. The rubbing was nice. My cheeks squeezed tightly on his cock.

The night before I left we quarrelled. Our words floated about, bubble-floating. They escaped through the door. His stepmother netted them. She entered and spoke to us. The oil lamps were still lit.

"I will bring you wine—you must be happy," she said. Her nightgown was pale and filmy. I could see her breasts. Balloons. I could see the dark blur of her pubis, her pubic hair, her wicked.

"Wine, yes—'twould be splendid," Edward said. He was pale and thin. Like his pintle. I had nursed it in my palm even while we quarrelled. It was the warm neck of a bird. I did not want it in my nest.

I heard his stepmother speaking to the maid downstairs. The maid was always up. There was clinking—bottle sounds, glasses sounds. We lay still, side by side. His stepmother returned and closed the door, bearing a tray. She poured wine We sat up like people taking medicine.

"Angela, dear, lie down," Edward said. His father had married her when Edward was fourteen. During the past months then of his father's absence in India, she had encouraged him to use her Christian name. I judged her about forty. A woman in full bloom.

Wine trickled and spilled on the sheet as she got in. Edward was between us—between the betweening of us. The ceiling grew higher. The sounds of our drinking sounded. The wine was suitably chilled. My belly warmed it. We were people in a carriage, going nowhere. We indulged ourselves in chatter. The bottle emptied quickly.

We must sleep, we must lie down, Angela said.

"I will stay with you until you sleep."

I heard her voice say that. The ceiling came down. It had never done that before. I passed my hand up into it and it was made of cloud. We lay down side by side on our backs. Our breathing came. There was warmth. Edward laid his hand on my thigh. He moved my nightgown up inch by inch. He touched. Into my fur, my nest, he touched. The lips were oily, soft. I did not move. His hand on the other side of him moved. I could feel the sheet fluttering there.

Our eyes were all open. I did not look but I knew. Soft, wet sounds. I tried not to move my bottom. Would the maid enter to remove the tray? Edward's fingertips found my button. I felt rich, forlorn, lost. My legs stretched down and widened. My toes moved. On the other side of him the sheet fluttered still.

Edward moved. His finger was oily with my oily. He moved on his hip and turned towards me. I felt the pronging of his prong. His hand cupped my nest.

"Kiss goodnight, Beatrice."

His voice was above me, yet far away—a husk blown on the wind. I moved my face sideways to his.

"Yes, kiss goodnight," Angela said.

Her voice was far away—a leaf floating on the sea. His mouth met mine. His charger quivered against my bared thigh. Fingers that were not my fingers ringed the stem of his cock. His finger entered me. I moved not. Our mouths were pasted together, unmoving. I was running through meadows and my father was chasing me. My mother and my sister, Caroline, were laughing. I screeched. Their voices drifted away on to the far horizon and waved there like small flags.

Moving my hand I encountered Angela's hand—the rings upon her fingers that ringed around his cock. I moved my mouth away from Edward's and stared up at the ceiling. It had gone high, gone high again. Birds drifted through it. Edward's hand eased my thighs wider. I lay limp, moist in my moistness. The bed quivered as if an engine were running beneath it.

I found my voice.

"Kiss goodnight," I said. My mind was not blank. There was coloured paper in it. A kaleidoscope. I watched the swirling, the patterns. Would love come?

Edward turned. His knob burned in his turning against my thigh. His nightgown was fully raised. His lips fell upon Angela's. Her hand held his cock still. At first she lay motionless. The sheet moved, tremored, rippled up and down. In her breathings were the secrets of the passageways at night.

Edward groaned in his groaning. The meshing of their lips. I heard their tongues. Voices.

"Edward—no, not now!"

They were speaking in ordinary speech.

"Oh, you bad boy!"

The sheet became tented. I felt the opening of her thighs—the warmth exuding from her thick-furred nest. Her bottom shifted, rucking the sheet, smack-bounce of flesh to flesh. Her knees bent. Between her thighs she encompassed him. Small wet sounds. Slithery sounds. I held my legs open. I was gone, lost. They did not know me. The bed heaved, shook. I turned my head. I looked as one looks along a beach at other people.

Did I know them?

Her nipples stood like tiny candles in brown saucers, laved by Edward's tongue. Her hands gripped his shoulders. Her eyes and lips were closed as if she were communing. Between her thighs his loins worked with febrile jerkings. Tiny squishing sounds. Her bottom began to move, jerking to his jerks.

Expressionless I moved the sheet down with my foot. It wrinkled, crinkled, slid away, betraying the curves of her calves. His mouth buried her mouth beneath his mouth. Her hands clawed his back. Their movements became more frenetic. The pale pistoning of his pintle cock.

Moaning in the night. Bliss of it. Was there bliss of it? I wanted to be held down. I wanted a straw to chew or a piece of long sweet grass whose root is white.

Angela was panting. It was a rough sound. The squelching of his indriving, outsucking. His balls smacked her bottom. The sound pleased me. Through their puffing cheeks the working of their tongues.

"Ah! dearest, let me come!"

Edward raised himself on forearms, loins flashing. Her hands clutched his arms. I was looking. Sideways along a cloud, a beach. The lamps were lit still. Had they forgotten the lamps?

"Oh, Edward!"

Kiss goodnight.

He collapsed, he shuddered, in his quivering quivered. Her calves rose and gripped his buttocks. A final thrust, indriven to the root. He seeped in his seeping, his jetting done. Like balloons bereft of air they collapsed. They were quiet. I could hear the ceiling. The floor creaked. Was the bed coming undone?

Edward rolled between us and was quiet. The night was done. The limp worm of his penis-pole lolled wet against my thigh. Sticky. It oozed. It was too small now for my nest.

In the night he stirred and mounted me. Drowsy in coils of sleep I did not resist. The oil lamps flickered low. Did she watch? From moment to moment I jerked my bottom in long memories of knowing. I wore drawers in my dreams. My bottom was being smacked. It was being smacked because there was a cock in me. In our soft threshings my legs spread. My ankle touched hers. She did not stir. Our feet rubbed gently together. Our toes were intimate.

Edward worked his work upon me and was done. The spurtings came in long, strong trills of warmth. Warm wet. Sperm trickled down my thighs. I lay inert. I had not come. He had not pleasured me. My nipples were untouched.

In the morning I left. Was that the reason? No. I do not know. Angela smiled at me and said. "It was the wine. We must make him happy." Her bottom was large and round beneath her peignoir. Edward kissed us. We took breakfast with the windows open.

I kissed them both when I left.

I was kind to them.

TWO

HOUSES seem smaller when one returns to them after a long period. The rooms shrink. They carry dead echoes. One looks for things one had left, but the drawers have been emptied. Furniture is moved. Even the small pieces of paper one had wished to keep have vanished. I like small pieces of paper. My notes to myself. Addresses, birthdays, anniversaries.

My notes to myself had all gone. Did I take them? Two reels of silk cotton that no longer matched my dresses lay in the back of a drawer in my dressing table. One was mauve and the other a pale blue. They were pretty. Once I used to keep biscuits in a jar on the top shelf of my wardrobe. Someone had eaten them. I told my sister Caroline.

"Beatrice, that was three years ago. You ate them," she

said. No one looked surprised. It was always a quiet house. We hate those who shout.

They knew I would come back.

"You should never have married," Father said. He looked at me sternly and added, "Did I not tell you? How old are you?"

"I am twenty-five," I replied, as if I were addressing a stranger. Dust swirled in the sunlight as I drew back the blue velvet curtains and raised the sash of my window.

"The maid does not clean," Father said. Did he see reproach in my eyes? He stood close to me and I could feel his bigness. The gold chain of his watch gleamed in the pale sun. There was a silence because we like silences. A baker's cart trundled down the street. From the side entrance of the house opposite a maid appeared, her white cap askew on her head. She raised her hand and the baker's man reined in his horse. A cat prowled by the railings.

Father stirred. He moved past me. His thighs brushed my bottom.

"I must return soon to Madras, Beatrice. You will have comfort here." His finger traced dust on the top of the rosewood cabinet by my bed.

"I shall be comfortable, Father. You will be gone long? Madras is so far."

"A year, my pet, and no more. Your Uncle Thomas will afford protection to you and your sister. Had you but returned before we might have walked with the early summer sun in the meadow."

"Yes, Father."

My uncle and my Aunt Maude lived close by. They had done so for years. We were close. Father's hand was upon my shoulder. I felt smaller. He stood behind me like a guard, a sentry. Did I like Uncle Thomas? I asked with my mind but not my mouth. They were brothers. There was kinship.

"Shall Jenny be there, too?" I asked. In my unmoving I asked. The baker's cart had rolled on with a tinkling of harness. The street lay quiet again as in a photograph. The maid had gone, loaf-clutching in her maidness, her maidenhood. Into a darkness of scullery, a glowering of gloom behind windows. Fresh smell of fresh bread.

"Jenny has grown as you have. You will like her more. She is fuller of form and pretty. In his guardianship of her your uncle has moulded her well," Father replied.

My buttocks moulded. Beneath my long silk dress they moulded. Proud in their fullness they touched his form lightly, gracing his grace with their curves. I felt the pressure of his being. There was comfort between us as in the days before my marriage. We had lain in the meadow and seen the flashing of wings, birds' wings, the butterflies. I leaned back. Father's hands touched my hair, the long gold flowing of my hair. The moulding of my bottom, ripe with summer.

"We shall drink wine. Come—let us celebrate your return," Father said.

I followed the first touch of his hand. We descended. The polished bannister slid smooth beneath my palm. Caroline waited on us, neat on a chaise-longue. At father's bidding she drew the bell-pull. The maid Sophie appeared. Wine was ordered.

In the coolness of its bottle glass it came. Father poured. The sofa received us. Like two acolytes we sat on either side of him. Sophie had gone. The door closed. In our aloneness we sat.

"We shall French-drink," Father said. It was a pleasantry we had indulged in before. I was but twenty-one then, Caroline seventeen. The wine glistened now again upon our lips. Our heads lay upon his shoulders. We sipped our sips while Father filled his mouth more deeply and turned his face to mine. His beard and moustache tickled. My parted lips received wine from his mouth. There was warmth. His hand lay on my thigh.

Father turned to Caroline. Foolishly shy she hid her face until her chin was raised. I heard the sounds, small sounds —the wine, the lips. A wasp buzzed and tapped against the window as if seeking entry, then was gone. The gardener chased the long grass with his scythe. I waited. The wine came to my mouth again. A whispering of lips. The ridging of my stocking top through my dress, beneath his palm. The tips of our tongues touched and retreated. Did the French drink this way? Father had been to Paris. In his knowing he had been.

Long did we linger. Caroline's dress rustled. I could not see. Across his form I could not see. The bottle emptied but slowly like an hour-glass. The wine entered my being. As through shimmering air Caroline rose at last, her face flushed. She adjusted her dress. Her eyes had a look of great foolishness.

"Go to your room, Caroline," Father said. There was yet wine in his glass. Silent as a wraith she was gone, her blushes faint upon the air like the smoke from a cigar.

"She is yet young," Father said. His tone was sombre. There was wine on my breasts once when I was eighteen and he had kissed it away. The wine made pools of goodness and warmth in me. It journeyed through my veins and filled my head.

"We shall go to the attic," Father said. His hand held mine—enclasped and covered it. As we rose his foot nudged the bottle and it fell. A last seeping of liquid came from its mouth. We gazed at each other and smiled.

"You will come, Beatrice? It is for the last time." There was a sadness.

We ascended, our footsteps quiet. The door to Caroline's room stood closed, thick in its thickness. The patterned carpet on the curving stair drank in our steps. Above the first floor were the guest rooms. In the old days those who wished had passed from bedroom to bedroom at nights during the long weekend parties my parents held. I knew this though my lips did not speak. At nights I had heard the whisperings of feet—a slither-slither of secrets. Arrangements were made discreetly with my mother as to the placings in rooms. The ladies of our circle always arranged such things. The gentlemen took it as manna. Bedsprings squeaked. I had told Caroline, but she did not believe me. There were moanings and hushed cries—the lapping sounds of lust. Small pale grey puddles on the sheets at morning.

No one had ever seen me go to the attic with Father. It was our game, our secret. Our purity.

In the attic were old trunks, occasional tables my mother had discarded or replaced, vases she disliked, faded flowers of silk. Pieces of unfinished tapestry lay over the backs of two chairs. Sunlight filtered through a dust-hazed window.

We entered by the ladder and stood. In the far corner near the dormer window stood the rocking horse, grey and mottled. Benign and handsome—polished in its varnished paint—it brooded upon the long gone days. Dead bees lay on the sill. In my kindness I was unhappy for them. Father's hand held mine still. He led me forward. My knees touched the brocaded cloth of an armchair whose seat had sagged. Upon it lay a mirror and a brush, both backed with tortoiseshell. They were as I had used of old up here.

Father turned his back to me and gazed out through the glass upon the tops of the elms. A trembling arose in me which I stilled. With slow care I removed my dress, my underskirt, and laid them on the chair. Beneath I wore but a white batiste chemise with white drawers whose pink ribbons adorned the pale of my thighs. My silk brown stockings glistened. I waited.

Father turned. He regarded me gravely and moved towards me. "You have grown. Even in three years you have grown," he said. "Where shall you ride to?"

I laughed. "To Jericho," I replied. I had always said that though I did not know where it was. Nodding, his hand sought the brush. I held the mirror. With long firm strokes of the bristles Father glossed and straightened my hair. Its weight lay across my shoulders, in its lightness. Its goldness shone and he was pleased.

"It is good," Father said, "the weather is fair for the journey. My lady will mount?"

We stepped forward. He held the horse's reins to keep it still. Once there had been a time when my legs could hold almost straight upon the horse. Now that I was grown more I had to bend my knees too much. My bottom slid back over the rear of the saddle and projected beyond the smooth grey haunches. Father moved behind me and began to rock the horse with one hand. With the other he smacked my outstretched bottom gently.

"My beautiful pumpkin—it is larger now," he murmured. My shoulders sagged. In the uprising of my bottom I pressed my face against the strong curved neck of the horse. It rocked faster. I clung as I had always clung. The old planked floor swayed and dipped beneath me. His palm smacked first one cheek and then the other.

"Oh! no more!" I gasped.

All was repetition.

"It is far to Jericho," my father laughed. I could feel his happiness in my head. The cheeks of my bottom burned and stung. My knees trembled. The bars of the stirrups held tight under the soles of my boots.

"No more, father!" I begged. His hand smacked on. I could feel the impress of his fingers on my moon.

"Two miles—you are soon there. What will you do when you arrive?"

"I shall have handmaidens. They will bathe and perfume me. Naked I shall lie on a silken couch. Sweatmeats will be brought. Slaves shall bring me wine. There shall be water ices."

I remembered all the words. I had made them up in my dreams and brought them out into the daylight.

"I may visit you and share your wine?" Father asked. His hand fell in a last resounding smack. I gasped out yes. I fell sideways and he caught me. He lifted me until my heels unhooked from the stirrups. I sagged against him. My nether cheeks flared. In the pressure of our embrace my breasts rose in their milky fullness above the lace of my chemise. My nipples showed. I clenched my bottom cheeks and hid my face against his chest.

"It was good. I should bring the whip to you henceforth," Father murmured.

The words were new. They were not part of our play. Beneath my vision I could see my nipples, the brown buds risen. Had I forgotten the words? Perhaps we had rehearsed them once. In their smallness they lay scattered in the dust. Dried flecks of spokenness.

"It would hurt," I said.

"No, it is small. Stand still." I did not know what to do with my hands. He was gone to the far corner of the attic and returned. In his hands was a soft leather case. He opened it. There was a whip. The handle was carved in ebony, the end bulbous. There were carvings as of veins along the stem. From the other end exuded strands of leather. I judged them not more than twenty-five inches long. The tapered ends were loosely knotted.

"Soon, perhaps. Lay it for now beneath your pillow, Beatrice."

So saying he cast aside the case and I took the whip. At the knob end was a silky smoothness. The thongs hung down by my thigh. A tendon stood out on my neck in my blushing. Father traced it with his finger, making me wriggle with the tickling. Broad trails of heat stirred in my bottom still. I could hear his watch ticking. The handle of the whip felt warm as if it had never ceased being touched.

I moved away from him. The thongs swung, caressing the sheen of my stockings. Father assisted me in the replacing of my dress. His hands nurtured its close fitting, smoothing it about my hips and bottom. His eyes grew clouded. I stirred fretfully. My hair was brushed and burnished anew. Father's mouth descended upon mine. His fingers shaped the slim curve of my neck.

"It was good, Beatrice. You are grown for it—riper, fuller. The smacks did not hurt?"

I shook my head, but then smiled and said "A little." We both laughed. In the past there had been wine afterwards, drawn from a cooling box that he had placed beforehand in the attic. Now we had drunk before and it moved within us.

His fingers charmed the outcurve of my bottom—its glossy roundness tight beneath my drawers. We kissed and spoke of small things. I would never come to the attic again, I thought. In the subtle seeking of our fingers there were memories. At last we descended. Father took the ladder first. Halfway down he stopped and guided my feet in my backwards descent. His hands slid up beneath my skirt to guide me.

Caroline was reading when we re-entered the drawing

room. Her eyes were timid, seeking, brimmed with questions.

"There is a new summerhouse—come, I will show you, Beatrice," Father said. I shook my head. I must see to my unpacking with the servant. Father would forgive me. His eyes forgave me. They followed me like spaniels, loping at my heels.

"Your boots are repolished—the spare ones," Caroline called after me. It was as if she meant to interrupt my thoughts. Father went to her and drew her up.

"Let us see if the workmen have finished in the summerhouse," he said.

Her eyes were butterflies on and on. I turned and stood of a purpose, watching her rising. Her form was as slender as my own. Her blue dress yielded to her springy curves. Through the window I watched them pass beneath the arbour. Three workmen in rough clothes came forward from where the new building stood and touched their caps. My father consulted his watch and spoke to them. After a moment they went on, passing round by the side of the house towards the drive and the roadway.

Their day was finished, or their work was done. Father seemed not displeased. Caroline hung back but he drew her on. Her foolishness was evident to me even then. The sun shone through her skirt, offering the outlines of her legs in silhouette. She was unmarried, but perhaps not untried. I fingered the velvet of the curtains, soft and sensuous to my touch. The lawn received their footsteps. The door to the summerhouse was just visible from where I stood. Father opened it and they passed within. It closed.

I waited, lingering. My breath clouded the pane of glass.

The door did not re-open. The shrubs and larches looked, but the walls of the summerhouse were blank.

Going upstairs to my room I fancied I heard a thin, wailing cry from Caroline.

THREE

WHEN Caroline smiles I know something, but I do not know what I know.

The whip lay untouched beneath my pillow. Father was due to depart. There was movement about the house. Trunks, valises. Two hansom cabs were needed—one for the luggage.

In the night before his departure I slipped my hand beneath my pillow and touched the whip, the smoothness of the handle, the coiling of the waiting thongs. My thumb traced the carved veins upon the penis shape. It moved to the knob, the swollen plum. After long moments of caressing it I got up and moved along the dark of the passageway. The door to father's bedroom was ajar. I stilled myself and took an extra pillow from the linen cupboard, making no sound.

The door to Caroline's room lay half open. Normally it was closed, as was mine at night. In the night. I peered within, expecting her to sit up. In the milky gloom she lay sprawled on her bed. Her hair was fanned untidily over her pillow. The hem of her nightdress was drawn up, exposing her thighs and the shadowy thatch of ash-blonde hair between. Her eyes were closed, lips parted.

I moved forward quietly, expecting to surprise her. She stirred not. Her legs lay apart in an attitude of lewd abandon. Slender fingers curled lax upon the innerness of her thigh—the firm flesh of pleasure there. Between the curls the lips of pleasure pouted. In the pale moonlight it seemed to me that there was a glistening there, as even upon her fingertips. Her breathing was the breathing of a child.

I stirred her shoulder with my hand. Drowsily her eyes opened.

"You are uncovered. Come—don't be naughty," I scolded. She prefers me in my scolding.

My hands slid beneath her calves, lifting them. As with the motions of a nurse I drew the sheet and blanket over her. Beneath her bottom cheeks a faintly sticky moisture. Throwing one arm over her eyes she mumbled something. Pieces of unfinished words.

"You were long in the summerhouse today," I said. She answered not. The defensive movement of her forearm tightened over her face. "We are bad," I said. Her legs moved pettishly beneath the sheet and then lay still. An owl hooted, calling to witches.

"Bad," Caroline husked. She was a child repeating a lesson. I bent and kissed her mouth. Her lips yielded and then I was gone.

The hours passed as white clouds pass. At three the next

afternoon Father departed. The gates lay open. The hansom cabs waited. The second carried his luggage piled high as if in retreat from days that were too long, too dry. In the hallway we were kissed, our bottoms fondled. There was affection. The cabmen waited. A smell of horses—manure and hay. A jingling of harness, clatter of wheels and he was gone. Gone to the oceans, the sea-cry and the vivid sun. The women would be bronzed, I thought. I would bronze my body—my nipples rouged, erect.

Caroline did not speak. Her pale fretting was evident. In the drawing room Sophie bobbed and called me M'am instead of Miss Beatrice. I was pleased. With the master gone I now was mistress. We would take tea, I said, but no cakes.

"I want cakes," Caroline said. Her look was sullen. I meant to punish her—perhaps for the summerhouse or for lying with her thighs apart on her bed. I knew not. We were like travellers whom the train has left behind. We drank unspeaking, our minds in clouds of yesterday. Sophie came and went, silent as on castors. Then the doorbell jangled. Its sound seemed to cross the halls, the rooms, and tinkle in the rockery beyond the windows.

Alice went, adjusting her cap but leaving her white apron askew. It was our uncle. Announced, he bowed benignly to us both. He was a man of slightly ruddy countenance, neither tall nor short, strong in his ways. He owned a small manufactory and numerous saddlers' shops that were scattered about the county. Sophie poured fresh tea. We spoke of Father.

"Jenny has come?" I asked. My voice was an echo of my voice in the attic. My uncle nodded. He adjusted the set of his waistcoat rather as Alice had adjusted her cap.

"She is settling," he announced. "Her training has been of use," I believe.

"Was she not teaching?" I ventured the question. His eyes passed over the fullness of my breasts and then upon Caroline's.

"They are one," he declared. "You will come for dinner."

It was not a question. I would have preferred it to be a question. His hazel eyes were like Father's. They sought, found and alighted. I felt their pressure upon my thighs.

"At eight," I said. I knew exactly at what hour they dined. I rose. "Uncle—if you will excuse me."

Politely, as I thought, he rose in unison with me. Caroline's glances hunted and dropped. "Let me accompany you," he said. It was unexpected. I desired to say that I was going to my room, but I suspected that he guessed. The moment was uncanny. It was as if Father had returned, shaven of his beard and wearing another suit. I could scarce refuse. At the door to my room I hesitated, but there was a certain urging in his look. The door closed behind us.

"Beatrice, you will bring the whip," my uncle said.

A bubble of *no* came to my lips, then sank again. That he knew of it seemed to me a treachery—bizarre, absurd. His expression nevertheless was kind. Without seeking an invitation he advanced upon me and embraced me. I leaned against him awkwardly. There was a tobacco smell. Memories of port.

"I have to care for you, nurture you, Beatrice. There are reasons."

I sought but could not find them. Delicately his fingertips moved down the small buttons at the back of my dress. My chin rested against the upper pocket of his coat. With some absurdity I wondered what was in it.

"The whip—it has many thongs, has it not?"

He raised my chin. My eyes swam in his seeing. My lips parted. Pearls of white teeth.

"Lick your lips, Beatrice—I desire to see them wet."

Unknowing I obeyed. He smiled at the pink tip of my tongue. It peeped like a squirrel and was gone. I was in another's body, and yet it was my own. We moved. I felt our moving. Backwards, stiffly. My calves touched the rolled edge of my bed. His right hand sought my bottom and slid beneath the bulge.

"Reach down and backwards for the whip. Beneath your pillow. Do not turn," he said. His fingers cupped my cheeks more fiercely. The blush rose within me. A tendon strained in my neck. Held about my waist by his other arm, I leaned back, I sought. My fingers floundered. He assisted me in my movements. The ebony handle came to my hand. It slipped. I gripped again. In a moment I held it by my side, still leaning back as I was told.

"It is good. You shall remain obedient, Beatrice, while in my care. Speak now, but do not move. I want you thus."

"And Caroline?" I asked. Were the secrets about to be unlocked? There were cracks in the ceiling. Tributaries. I knew not what I spoke.

"It shall be. You must be trained. Upright now—come! hard against me!"

I wilted, twisted, but to no avail. A hand forced into my back brought me up, slamming against him. My breasts ballooned. His hand supported my bottom. Father had not treated me this way. I had come to his arms and said nothing. In the attic we had whispered secrets, but they were small.

The root of manhood was against me. Against my belly. I would have swooned save for his clasp. Then of a sudden he released me and I fell. Backwards upon my bed. Forlorn as a child. The whip dangled its thongs across my knees.

"At eight," my uncle said. The bulge in his britches was considerable. I had seen it in father's but had averted my eyes. I hung my head. There was a loneliness within me that cried for satisfaction. I said yes—hearing my voice say yes. My nipples stung their tips beneath my bodice.

My uncle departed, leaving gaps in the air. I rose and gazed down from the window as I had gazed with Father. A woman in black carrying a parasol walked past holding the arm of a man. The cry of a rag-and-bone merchant came to my ears, long away, far away. In a distant cave. Below there were voices. Mumblings of sound. Why did Caroline always cry out? How foolish she was. I sat again, fondling the whip. In the attic I would have received it, I knew. The horse would have rocked. My pumpkin raised, bursting through my drawers. I had shown Father my nipples. We were bad.

In the morning I would be alone, walking through the clear air.

My bottom had not tasted the whip. I turned before my dressing-table mirror and raised my skirts. Perhaps I would cease to wear drawers. Their frilled legs were pretty. Pink ribbons dangled their brevity against the milky skin of my thighs. Awkwardly I slashed the thongs across my cheeks. The sting was light.

I wanted to go to Jericho—to lower my drawers and let my pubis show. The curls were soft, springy and thick. The thongs would flick within my groove. I would clutch the horse's neck, the dappled grey, the shine of him, and cry. I would cry tears of wine. The dead bees upon the windowsill would stir. "All shall be well with the best of all possible bottoms," Father had said to me once. We had laughed.

"Pangloss," I declared. I knew my Voltaire. Pangloss and bottom gloss, Father said. There was purity.

I repaired my disorders of dress and brushed my hair. I am never given to allowing servants to do it. In the drawing room Caroline sat as placidly as she would have me believe she always did. I needed to challenge her. I went and sat beside her. She was surprised, I believe, at my composure.

"Did Uncle kiss you?" I asked. She shook her head. Her cheeks were bright red. "Or feel your thighs?" I added. Her gasp sounded within my mouth as I drew back her neck and kissed her. My hand sought her corsage. There was a loose button.

Her nipples were stiff.

Loosing second and third buttons, my small hand squeezed within. The jellied mounds of her breasts were firm and full—only a trifle smaller than my own. Caroline struggled, but I am stronger than she. She endeavoured to raise her arms between us but the enclosure of my arm was too tight. Her lips made petal shapes of helplessness. Her breath was warm. My hand slipped down, cupping the luscious gourd. The ball of my thumb flicked the nipple.

"Between your thighs, Caroline," I murmured. I did not say of what I spoke, nor of whom I spoke. Her head shook violently. Her eyes were lighthouses. "In your mouth? The smooth, hot knob?" I teased. Her expression became rigid with surprise. Her head fell back. I licked my tongue along her teeth and laughed. I released her, leaping to my feet. "How foolish we are!" I laughed. I turned and went before my disguise melted. I had never taken it in my mouth.

Caroline's mouth was so often petulant. It would have fitted perfectly. The rose and the stalk. I would have hidden and watched her sin. The delicate oozing of her mouth upon the rampant conqueror—balls pendant on her cupping palm. Her eyes would be half closed, lashes fluttering. The cock would jerk faster and she would choke. A warning hand would seize her head. Her cheeks would bulge as the penis urged deeper. Strong loins would work against her unwillingness.

And the spouting. He would have needed to cup her face completely—hold it in. Ripe throbbing of the flesh.

"Suck, Caroline." His voice would be deep and urgent, her head squeezed, ripplings of blonde hair through his fingers. Beneath her dress her breasts would lilt.

There was sin here, among the rubber plants, the rooms overcrowded with furniture, photographs of sepia in silver frames upon the piano. From the conservatory whence I fled I gazed upon the waving fronds of ferns. Father's train would have reached the terminal. His bags would be carried. The boat train at Liverpool Street would await him. Women would peer through carriage windows at his coming. Blinds would be drawn, expressions adjusted. The women would wear fine kid gloves, velvet-smooth to the touch on sensitive skin. Balls pendant. Veins.

"Suck, Caroline, suck."

Sperm is thick, salty. Once I tasted it on my palm. My sprinklings are salty when I sprinkle. Over the cock that is more powerful and thick than my husband's was. That is *now*. It was not *then*.

In my then I was alone in my aloneness. I returned to Caroline. She had not moved save to button her dress. The servant would enter soon with the oil lamps. Caroline stared down at the carpet and would not raise her eyes. I knew her moods. I sank to my knees and pressed my lips upon her thigh.

"Do not!" she said. Her voice was as distant as the far whistling of a train.

Kid gloves. The blinds drawn. Penis rampant. The knob of my whip. "There is no sin. Is there sin?" I asked Caroline. Sin once had been giggling in Sunday School. Now there was desire between our thighs.

"I do not know," Caroline said. Her voice fell like a small flake of metal. She was angry with me.

My desire became muted. I wanted to protect her. Soon, after we had bathed and changed for dinner, it would be almost eight o'clock. I looked up and she was staring at me.

Perhaps she knew her fate as well as I.

FOUR

AUNT MAUDE awaited us. She wore a black velvet choker. It suited her, I thought. Her dress swept back in a long train that was very modish. Her hair was piled high. Diamond earrings glittered.

My aunt was of a stature an inch taller than myself and full of form. Her breasts and bottom jutted aggressively. I took her for forty—younger than my uncle. Her eyes were kind but imperious. Though both were close to my father, neither Caroline nor I had spoken much with them through the years. Those of under age were always considered best unheard.

I spoke of Jenny. I was eager to see her. For a year we had shared a boarding school together.

"Later," my aunt said. The dining room table was

candlelit. My aunt preferred it to the smell of oil. Electricity had not then reached out from London and it was said that we were too far from the county town for gas pipes to be laid. Three years later magic would be wrought and they could come. My initiations—though I knew it not that evening—were to be by oil lamps in the old tradition. Frisky young ladies of Society were weaned on a bed with their drawers down, it was crudely said. Of cottage life and that in other dowdy dwellings, we knew nothing except, as we understood, that the males rutted freely.

Although married, and now separated, I still obtained innocence in many degrees, as shall be seen. At dinner my aunt and uncle spoke to us as if the past were still upon us. My aunt tutted severely when Caroline spilled a drop of wine. The servant was called of a purpose to mop it up.

"You will stay the night," my aunt said after coffee had been taken. We sipped liqueurs and said nothing. Jenny had still not appeared. I wondered anxiously if she ate in her room. Had she been whipped? She had come to them in childhood—or rather, to my uncle first. An orphan, it was said. One did not know. I sought for strength to object, to rise, to leave, but their eyes were heavy upon me.

At ten-thirty my aunt looked at the clock. "Tom, you will take her up," she said. My palms moistened. I knew of whom she spoke, though she had not the delicacy to use my name. Caroline said nothing. Would she not save me?

The house was as ours except that the interior pattern was reversed. Perhaps that was symbolic. The stairs were on the left, as one entered the hall, instead of on the right. Entering as I had first done I had placed the whip somewhat furtively behind the large mahogany stand in the hall which carried occasional cloaks and walking sticks.

"Go to your room and I will follow," my uncle said. I had been shown it briefly already. It lay as my own lay on the first floor. Left to right it was a mirror image. The curtains were brown, the drapes edged with ivory tassels. The air tremored. The furniture looked at me. I wanted the room to go away, the walls to dissolve, the air to take me high, free, upfloating in the blue dark of night. The carpet rolled beneath me like the sea. I moved, and moved towards the bed. Two pillows were piled high upon a bolster. Was my whip there?

I would not seek it. I refused. This was not my room. As by habit I opened a small wall cabinet and found to my surprise that which I kept in my own—a bottle of liqueur and two small glasses. Pleasure traced itself across my lips and then was gone. I turned, closing the cabinet. My uncle had entered. In his hand he held the whip. Moving he moved, towards me moved. He took my hand, the palm of mine, sheened with moisture.

"Beatrice, bend over—hands flat on the quilt."

"Uncle—please!"

My mouth quivered. I did not want it to be my mouth. His hand reached out caressing my neck and I gave a start. His fingers moved, soothing.

"You will obey, Beatrice."

The world was not mine. Whose was the world? Would Caroline and my aunt discuss me?

"No one will come," my uncle said. The door stood solid. We were on an island. In the attic Father and I had stood on the top of the world. The whip moved. He passed the handle around and beneath the globe of my bottom, shaping, carving. His lips nuzzled my neck. I could not run.

"Uncle—please, no!"

I broke from him and stood trembling. The thongs swayed down to his knee like a fall of rain in slow motion. His eyes were kind. His arm reached out. He took my chin and raised it.

"There are things you need, Beatrice. There are locked rooms above. There are keys."

I did not want to blink in the meeting of our eyes. Go into the world clear-eyed and so return from it.

"Yes?" I asked. There was imperiousness in my voice. Dare I rebel? The whip slipped from his grasp and fell upon the patterned carpet. He would not whip me. He could not. I knew it. I felt happy. He waited further upon my speech, my quest, my questions.

"What is in the rooms?" I asked.

He took my hand. We walked. The stairs received us. Caroline had wandered perhaps into the dark garden—into the long grass which the gardener chased by day. The grass would receive her. Her eyes would be loam, her nipples small blossoms. Her pubic hair would be moss. There was silence below in the house. Along the passageway of the second floor as we went my uncle rattled keys. A door opened.

The attic! They had made a replica of it! Except for the dormer window—but it did not matter. The door closed—a heavy click—we were alone. My uncle's arm encircled my shoulder. I could not speak. Let me speak.

"The horse is the same. Only the horse, Beatrice."

It was true. Trunks, boxes, broken pieces of furniture, old vases—all lay as they might have lain in our house.

His hand stroked my back, warm through my gown.

"Go to the horse, Beatrice."

I moved, walked, threading my way among the tumbled things—the love things, the loved things. The horse was large, bright, new. The stirrups gleamed, the saddle and the reins shone. The mottled, dappled grey was the same. I stroked the mane. On my own horse the mane was worn and thin where I had too often grasped it, but here it was new and thick. The leather smelled of new leather. Heady.

For a last moment I turned and looked towards the closed door. Caroline into the long grass gone. At breakfast she would return. Out of the caves of my dreams she would return, pure in her purity, the loam fallen from her eyes, her nipples budding, the moss of her pubis gold and curled.

I waited, humbled in my waiting. The sea moved beneath Father. The timbers of the sailing ship would creak. The dark waters. Kid gloves soiled with sperm upon the waves. Salt to sperm. The licking lap of water.

Hands at my back. I did not stir. My uncle unbuttoned. The sides of my gown fell from my shoulders. The material dragged to my waist and heaped. I stood still. His hands savoured the outswell of my bottom, raising the skirt. My drawers were bared. A lusciousness of thighs. I fancy myself upon the silkiness of my skin.

"Mount," my uncle said. I raised my leg. The skirt slip-slithered down again, enfolding my legs. As if tired my leg fell again. "Remove your dress," he breathed.

I wanted blindness but found none. The oil lamps, ranged around the room, flickered. Small messages of lambent light. My hair ruffled as I stripped off my gown. There was no one to brush it. My underskirt fell to my ankles. I stepped out of it as out of foam. Sperm-foam. The dark sea lapping. Silent in a cabin, my thighs apart.

Cupping my bottom as I toed the stirrup, my uncle assisted me in my rising.

He knew not of Jericho. There were secrets still. The horse jolted, moving as if on springs rocking. The movement was smooth as velvet, soundless. I clung to the neck. My brazen bottom reared, my pumpkin warm.

"Ah!" I gasped at the first smack, and the next. There was a sweetness in the stinging I had known before. Because of my excitement perhaps. Was I excited? My hips squirmed to his palming smacks, my back dipped. I clung, I

squeezed the cheeks, I squealed. Would Caroline hear? Under the deep lush grass would Caroline hear?

At the tenth smack—lifted down—I foundered, falling, grasped in his strong grasp. Words tumbled, spun like pellets in a drum. Words polished in their spinnings. Hands clasped my bulging cheeks. I blushed, I hid my face. His fingers drew the cheeks apart beneath my drawers. I strove to be still as Father so oft had taught me. My heels teetered. Then I managed it.

"So," my uncle said. He was satisfied. I closed my eyes, pretending myself in the attic. I was happy. The stinging in my bottom had made tears glint in my eyes. "You are older now, Beatrice—it is better."

I wanted wine. I wanted to go down to Caroline, to rescue her from the long grass. My uncle held me. My nipples peeped.

"Is it not better, Beatrice?"

Was I to answer? I knew not. I believe he expected it not. My silence pleased him. He sought confusion, girlishness there. My bottom cheeks weighed heavy on his palms.

"Raise your arms, Beatrice, and place them behind your head."

It was a game—a new game. I obeyed. My left elbow nudged his cheek. His breath was warm on my face. I was obedient. We had never done this in the attic. Once on Christmas Eve in the merriment of the night I had been carried up to my room, my drawers removed. Had I dreamed that? Tomorrow I would buy kid gloves, long and white to my elbows. The kid leather would be of the finest. Sensitive to flesh. A stem upstanding.

My uncle raised my chemise inch by inch. I was naked beneath. I quivered. My hips would not keep still. He raised it, raised it to the silky melons of my breasts. And then above. Dark nipples in their radiant circles.

"No!"

I jerked, twist-tumbled, gasped. I did not want to be obedient. The lacy hem of my chemise tickled my nipples in its rising.

"Uncle, no!"

I cried, I fell. There was carpet on the floor—purple with dull red patterns. In the attic there was no carpet. Dust rose to my nostrils. My chemise was crumpled over my polished gourds, my tits, my breasts.

My uncle fell beside me. His hands pinned my shoulders. Gazing upon my gourds he gazed. He bent. His long tongue licked my nipples. My back reared but he stilled it with a warning grip of hands.

"Shall you be whipped?" he asked.

My eyes were mirrors. They encompassed the world. I stared at him in my staring. My hair flowed upon the carpet. I must have looked a picture of extreme wantonness. There was wet on my nipples where he had licked. They strained in the rising. The floor moved gentle under me as waves beneath a tall ship sailing. In Madras the women would be bronzed, their hips supple.

"Lift your hips," my uncle said.

My heels dug into the carpet. For a moment I lay mutinous. Then my knees bent, bottom lifted. I was arched. His fingers sought the ties of my drawers, the pretty ribbons. Loosing they surrendered. Closing my eyes I felt my drawers being removed. The whorl of my navel showed. The impress of a baby's finger dipped in cream. Curls glinted at my pubis.

Then there was a sound.

The door had opened and a young woman stood there in a severe black costume. The toes of her black boots shone.

It was Jenny.

FIVE

JENNY took me to my room. I carried my dress. The ribbons of my drawers had been tied again on my rising when she appeared. My uncle had risen and kissed her brow.

"We were playing games," I said. I sat on the bed. I wondered how Jenny had arrived. Perhaps she had been here all the time hiding behind the wallpaper—a voice in the shrubbery. Owl calls. Night calls. She looked older, younger—both. The appearance of her costume was severe—high buttoned to her neck. Her face was Byzantine. By Giotto perhaps. Her long thick hair was swept back and tied with a piece of velvet.

"Games are nice," Jenny said. She came and sat close to me, legs together, hands in her lap. I felt comforted. Had I betrayed myself upstairs? My uncle had followed us to the door, avuncular. Jenny was talking. There were words. I caught her words in the broad net of my mind.

"You must be kind to him, Beatrice. We must all be kind."

"Have you just come?" I asked. My hands had not trembled. My voice was bright and clear. In the room with my uncle I had been speechless, mumbling. How foolish. The skin of my breasts beneath the low neck of my chemise was glossy, tight and full. Jenny looked at them. I saw her look. We used to undress together—when I stayed with her. When she stayed with me. But then I remembered something. Something I had never believed in.

One weekend when she had come to stay, six or seven years before, Mother had said to me, "It is best if Jenny has the guest room tonight." Jenny had looked strange, I thought—sitting, listening. She had nodded at me lightly as if she wanted me to say Yes.

I had heard sounds in the night, that night. It was midnight. I had looked at the clock—the small clock that says yes to me when I want it to be a certain time. There were sounds. Sounds like leather smacking. I thought I heard Jenny whimpering. The servants sometimes made noises in the night in their moving. But now the servants, too, would be abed.

A voice said, "You are a good girl, Jenny." It sounded like my mother's voice. My dreams were often strange. I sat up in bed. There were more leather sounds, little cries, a voice like Father's voice. The sounds and the voices stirred and were mixed. I heard a woman-voice murmur: "More—harder—a little harder. Ah, how sweet she looks."

Oh, a little scream I heard, a screamy-moan, then quiet. Sounds of breath like rushing waters. Bedsprings tinkled. Small bells of the night. Two men went past the house below—rough men, not from our neighbourhood. One shouted and I lost the sounds.

"I just came," Jenny said now. "There are clothes in your wardrobe. Have you looked?"

She drew me up. The mirrored doors, whose mirrors were tarnished, opened. From a shelf Jenny took black stockings of silk with a raised, ornate pattern that was run through with hints of silver. With it she produced a tiny waist corset of satin black. The small fringe of lace at the top that would fall beneath my breasts was silver, too. From the bottom of the wardrobe she drew out long high boots of the finest leather. The studs around which the laces wound were silver. The heels were slender, tall.

"Where is Caroline?" I asked.

Her eyes were glitter stones.

"You will look beautiful in these, Beatrice. Who?"

"Caroline."

"Yes, I know. Remove your chemise, stockings and shoes. Put these on."

She held them to me as a gift. I took them. The boots were light in weight. They would reach up to my thighs.

"It is late," I said. I licked my lips. My uncle had wanted to see my lips wet. Jenny did not smile. She raised my chemise and drew it off my head. I shook my hair like a dog emerging from water. As carefully as if I were a nervous yearling she knelt and drew off my drawers, my shoes. Without my shoes my thighs looked plumper.

"Your pubis is full—a splendid mound," she said. "You are beautiful, Beatrice. Your hips have the violin curve that men adore."

"I want to go home," I said. I felt sullen. Caroline's face was my face. My lips brooded.

"You will be good," Jenny said. She tickled me. She knew I hated being tickled. I squirmed, laughed, my breasts jiggled. I fell back on the bed, I rolled. She smacked my bottom. I yelped. The bright spreading of her fingers was upon it. It was a superb bottom, she said, the cleft as deep as a woman's heart. Her hands fell and pressed on it so that I could not rise. Her knee came into the small of my back.

"You will dress, Beatrice. You are not naughty, are you?"

"No," I said. She had seen Uncle taking down my drawers. My pubis had been offered. On her entry into the room upstairs he had stopped and risen as if we had merely been conversing. "What did you do in my parents' room?" I asked.

"What?" she asked sharply. She did not know my thoughts, my memories. Her palm tingled across my bottom again. "Dress!" she commanded me, "I like you in stockings best. You have the thighs for it—plumpish, sweet. Do not disobey. Get up!"

I obeyed her. The long boots were at first difficult to manage. They were tight. Their tops fell but three inches below the dark bands of the stocking tops. I would have difficulty in walking in them, I said. The corset nipped my waist. My hips blossomed. The corset framed my navel beneath an upward curve. My belly gleamed white.

"You will walk in them slowly and with stately tread —that is their purpose, Beatrice. Try."

I moved from her. I walked. The high heels teetered. My legs were constrained. I felt the movements of my bottom, naked.

"Stand!" she commanded me. I stood, my back to her. She drew upon my wrists and brought them behind my back. A metal clink—a clink of steel. My wrists were bound. I wanted to cry and hide my face. Next she secured my ankles. Why?

"Lie down, Beatrice."

I was bundled on to the bed, face down. "I don't want to," I said. I did not know what I meant. Jenny tut-tutted and arranged the tops of my stockings above the rimming leather. My toes were cramped in the boots. Jenny turned my face and bent and kissed my mouth. Full lips. Rose lips. She straightened and her eyes were solemn, full of night.

"You will stay so a little while," she told me. She moved away. A chinking of metal as I tried to move.

"Please don't, Jenny."

She was at the door. "I always loved you, Beatrice," she said.

"Please don't, Jenny."

She did not hear. The door closed. I was alone with my aloneness. In the night. Where was Caroline? I listened as I listened when a child, on evenings when the curtains were drawn in my room against the evening light. I listened now, I heard. There were footsteps, soft voices. Voices heard, unheard. Was it the wind? I was half naked and bound, strange in my half-nudity and bonds. Jenny was naughty. She would come and release me and I would dress in my summer dress and we would picnic. Caroline would be tied to a tree. She would watch our small white teeth nibbling cakes. Lemonade would gurgle down our throats. The world would never come to an end.

Did Caroline remove her chemise in the attic?

I heard voices. Caroline's voice. She was laughing. Jenny was laughing. I knew I must not call out in my calling. They stopped outside my door and went on up. I imagined in my imaginings my uncle waiting for her in the attic room.

It was quiet again. The walls are thick. I dozed. Tight in my bonds I dozed. The door opened. Was it a dream? Through slits of eyelids I saw Jenny. She was dressed as I was dressed save that there was no silver in her stockings nor in her corset. She wore drawers of black satin, but they had no legs. Their lines swept up between her thighs.

Aunt Maude entered behind her. The door was closed. From her ears dangled rubies in long gold pendants. Her mouth was carmine. In her hand the whip.

Was she an aunt? There were aunts in the garden once when I was young. They moved among the flowers and the shrubs. Sometimes Father and Mother would kiss them. We ate delicacies from silver platters. The servants were quiet, moving like wraiths. Tea was drunk from translucent cups. It was said that my uncle's first wife had left and died. I believe not that she died, but that she left I knew. Long later I heard of it. Her name was Lucy. She was but eighteen. My uncle then was a racier man. He sought a sexual abandonment to which Lucy could not lend herself. She was beautiful but shy. In the end my uncle grew impatient. He had wished to see her in the throes of lust. She had refused. One night, becoming impatient, he had called the butler. Lucy, naked, had been held down over the edge of the bed. First my uncle and then the butler had entered their penises in her bottom and buggered her. The butler was a lewd, crude man. Such things were not unknown. My uncle, it appeared, had been in raptures over the scene. He having buggered Lucy first, she was more docile and receptive to the second breaching of her bottom. Nevertheless, she departed soon after. For Australia, they said. Her death being announced, but never proved, my uncle remarried.

Aunt Maude sat now on the bed. I felt her weightness. She rolled me onto my hip, my back to her. Her hand caressed my cheek and brushed my hair back where the strands were loose.

"Has she been good?" she asked.

Jenny stood as if she had been waiting to be asked. "She

has been good," she said. I was pleased. They were going to release me. We would have our picnic. Jenny and I would hide in the shrubbery and Caroline would have to find us.

"It will take time," my aunt said. Her complexion was as smooth as mine. Once when I was very young she was younger. She bent over me so that our mouths almost touched. Jenny stood still. I knew that Jenny was being good standing still.

"She was smacked," Jenny said. I wanted to cry. I hated her. I glared at her and she smiled. My aunt continued to stroke my face and hair. Then she passed her long-tapered fingers down my neck and back. I shivered. I jerked towards her. Her eyes were kind.

"Twenty-five. She looks younger—she could be younger. Beatrice always had a fine bottom, did you not, Beatrice?"

My eyes said no-yes. Her fingertips floated my globe, my split peach, my pumpkin glory pale. The tip of her forefinger sought the groove. My lips quivered. Jenny did not look away. All hands should be hidden from people. My mother told me that. Hands can be wicked. My wrists were bound.

My aunt's finger tasted the inrolling of my bottom cheeks and wormed between them.

No—even my husband did not do that. Edward never did that. His stepmother was jealous of me. He bought her flowers. I remembered his cock. It was thin and long.

I made a noise—soft, small noise. The fingertip had touched my rose, my anus, my little bottom mouth that makes an O. My aunt smiled. She had turned my chin towards her. I bubbled little bubbling sounds. I jerked my bottom. My lips pursed in a long, soundless *oooooh*. The fingertip oozed in me and it moved. Back and forth, an inch of it, it moved.

My aunt took my nose pinched between her thumb and finger. I was like a fish. I had to part my lips to breathe. Rouge-scented, her mouth came to my mouth. Her tongue extended, licked within. I squirmed. Between my bottom cheeks her finger sank. In deeper sank. I was impaled. My breath hush-rushed. Her tongue worked. It worked its long wet work around my tongue. Her finger moved in-out, gently, like a train uncertain at a tunnel. Menace of dark and tightness.

Her finger felt burny, itchy, strange. Then it came out. Her tongue came out. I tasted her rouge on my mouth with my rouge. I wanted to tell Jenny that but I hated her. My aunt gave my bottom a pat and stood up. She smoothed her skirt down.

"She should bathe," my aunt said. "Take her, Jenny."

Jenny made me get up. Into the hallway I was led, along to the bathroom. As in those days it was huge—a fireplace within. The walls were draped with dark blue velvet all around. The bath was of white porcelain. Unshackled, my attire was removed. The water had already been brought in and emptied by the servants into the bath. It was lukewarm and pleasant.

"You know I love you," Jenny said.

I sat down. The water lapped me with its tongues. I liked that. Jenny sponged me and poured scented water over me from a pitcher.

"Do you remember we learned wicked words at boarding school?" she asked. I wanted to ask things, but I did not. I nodded. Her eyes were bright and merry. Christmas tree decorations. "What is *cunt?*" she asked.

"*Con,*" I said. I did not want her to think I did not know. I like the French word but not the English word. The English word is ugly. Its edges are sharp.

"And *prick?*" She held my head round so that I could

look into her eyes. Her breasts were splashed with water. I wanted to nibble her nipples.

"*Pine.*" I knew I was right. I would never then say prick. Why are all wicked words sharp in English? Someone sharpened them. Anglo-Saxons with dirty beards and guttural voices sharpened them. My bottom squashed its cheeks into the water, plump. Is it too big?

"And sperm?" She would not stop. Jenny was often like that before, not ever stopping. She would tickle me in bed when we were younger and make me say things. In my imaginings I would say better things, naughtier things, but I never told her. Did she know? Was this punishment?

"*Foutre,*" I said. I knew she liked the word best. I liked the word best. It was like a ripe plum being chewed and then pieces coming out briefly on the lips before being swallowed. The word was thick bubbles around my tongue. Creamy bubbles.

"Have you not been whipped yet?"

It was Jenny asking me. At first I did not know that it was. I thought the voice came from the ceiling. I did not answer. I was mute. Her fingers moved over the outjutting of my breasts. My nipples had risen under the sponge. Jenny licked inside my ear. I giggled. It wasn't fair.

"I knew you hadn't been," she said, "get up."

My feet slipped. She smacked me. "Now stand still," she said, just as Father and Uncle said. She sponged my legs and made me open them. The sponge was squelchy and warm under my pussy. Did Jenny ever touch me there before? No, yes. In bed once, I think. That was summers ago. The ice cream has all been eaten since then, the plates put away.

"Move your hips. Rub them against the sponge, Beatrice. Did you often come over Edward's prick?"

"I hate you," I said. There were tears in my eyes. She

knew that I would not tell her. She became impatient with me.

"Oh, get out," she said. She pulled me roughly from the bath and towelled me. She was brisk and quick as Mother used to be when I was young. Younger young. Then she powdered me. Clouds of powdering me. The powder made me sneeze.

She led me back into my room. The house was silent. Had they all run away?

"I want champagne," I said. I do not know why I said it. Bubbles. *Foutre*. Jenny laughed.

"There should be rouge on your nipples," she said. She had left the door open. From along the passageway came sounds, cries, whimpers.

"Please?" I asked. I felt as if I were speaking in a foreign language and that I only knew the beginnings of sentences. Then I recovered myself. "I heard Caroline," I said.

Jenny put a white linen nightdress over my head. It flowed to my feet. The hem was wide. "You shall see," she replied. She took my hand and led me along the corridor. The door to Caroline's room was half open.

Caroline was lying naked on her bed, face down. Her wrists and ankles were bound as mine had been. Aunt Maude was swishing a long slender cane lightly across her tight, pink cheeks. Caroline's face was flushed. At every contact of the cane she jerked her hips and whimpered.

"You will both sleep now," Jenny said. She pushed me back into my room and closed the door. I heard the lock click. The tasselled curtains parted to my hands. I pressed my forehead to the cool glass and stared down into darkness. The baker's van had gone—the maid—the cat. Had the loaf been eaten?

My bed was soft and comfortable, the sheets scented with lavender. The oil lamps made shadows on the ceiling. I could not stir myself to extinguish them. A servant would come in the morning and attend to them.

Through the green-blue sea I floated. The dark shadow of a huge ship loomed above me. I reached and touched the planks and felt the barnacles. There was seaweed in my hair. Father came floating towards me. My skirts billowed up to my hips in the deep, still waters.

No one could see.

SIX

THE sun was warm when I awoke. The curtains had been drawn back—the lamps removed. Evidently I had slept heavily. Jenny roused me, smiling from the doorway where she stood. The gong below sounded for breakfast.

"You are late," she said. She wore a long black skirt, the waist drawn in tight. Her blouse was white, the buttons of pearl. Beneath the silk of her blouse, her breasts loomed pinkly. A perking of nipples. They indented the material. Like a child late for school I was hustled into the bathroom and out again.

"I have no dress to wear," I said. Jenny smacked my hand.

"You are late," she repeated. The smell of sizzling bacon came to us. I was hungry. My mouth watered. The wardrobe doors were opened quickly. A thin wool dress of light brown colour, rust colour, was handed to me. "Nothing beneath except your stockings," Jenny said. She palmed my bottom and my breasts as I raised my nightdress. The sensation was pleasant. The dress cascaded over my shoulders and was worked tightly down over my curves. It was as if I were naked. I was preferred in boots today, Jenny said —black lace-up ones that came to my knees. The heels were high. I feared to fall down the stairs. I told her.

"Nonsense," Jenny said. "Brush your hair quickly. Show me your teeth. Are they clean now?"

I was taken down. Approaching the dining room we walked more slowly. My legs felt longer in the boots, the high heels. My aunt and uncle and Caroline were already seated. Silver tureens stood on the massive sideboard. Caroline looked up at me quickly and then attended to her bacon. We ate in silence as if some doom were pending. Neither my aunt nor uncle spoke, even to one another. It was a penance perhaps. I ate voraciously but delicately. The bloom of health was upon me. The kidneys and mushrooms were delicious. The maids who served were young and pretty. I liked them. They avoided my eyes. They had learned their learning.

With every movement of Jenny's body her breasts moved their nipples beneath her blouse. Beneath the tablecloth my uncle's hand stole onto her thigh. She wore garters that ridged themselves slightly through her skirt. He caressed them. His palm soothed from one leg to the other. Jenny parted her legs beneath her skirt and smiled. I wanted to suck the tip of her tongue.

At a nod from my uncle we were dismissed. Caroline and I rose together and wandered into the drawing room. We were lost in our foundness. We held hands. Our fingers whispered together. In a moment, from a side entrance, my uncle appeared in the garden. A carriage had arrived, it seemed, but the visitors came not to the front of the house. They skirted the side and appeared where my uncle stood.

The woman whom he greeted was in her early thirties. I had a vagueness of seeing her before. Her flowered hat was large, of pale straw with a wide brim. She wore white kid gloves to her elbows. Were they my gloves? I had left mine in the sea at night. The fishes had nibbled at them. She was beautiful, elegant. Her dress was of white and blue, the collar frilled. Pearls glinted around the neck. Beside her came a servant neatly dressed in black with velour lapels to his jacket. He had an air of insolent subservience.

"She is beautiful," I said to Caroline, "do you know who she is?"

Jenny's voice sounded behind us. "What are you doing?" she asked in a sharp tone. A tone that scratched.

"I was asking," I answered.

Caroline moved. Her palm was moist in mine. "I know her. She is Katherine Hayton—an actress. We have seen her at the Adelphi," she said. Her eyes were saucers as she received Jenny's stare.

"You were not told to hold hands," Jenny said. She jerked her head at me and said, "Come. Beatrice, come."

Forlorn, I relinquished Caroline's hand. Our own house was yet an ocean away. In the bedrooms women with bronzed skins and supple hips were lying. They would wear my clothes and steal my jewellery.

Jenny led me down the hall. To my astonishment we entered the linen room. It smelled of starch and nothing. "You must learn—you must both learn, Beatrice. Do you not know?" Jenny asked me.

I blinked. I did not know who I was. Father had lied perhaps. He had not gone to Madras. He was with the women in the rooms. They would French-drink. Their lips would taste of curry. There would be musk between their thighs. I said yes to Jenny. My voice said yes. My hands were at my sides.

"Kneel before me, Beatrice."

I did. My head was bowed, my hands clasped together. I prayed for goodness. Edward's mother used to undress with her door half open. We could see her as we went past. Her bottom was big. I told Edward that she should close the door. He smiled. His eyes were small and neat. Like his *pine* when it was not stiff.

"Kiss my thighs," Jenny said. She raised her skirt, gathering up the folds. I was blind. A milkiness, a perfume. Her drawers were split both back and front. It was the fashion then. Women could attend to their natural functions without removing them. In my mother's early days women had never worn drawers.

The curls of her slit, her loveslot, honeypot, were framed by the white linen. My palms sought the backs of her thighs. Her knees bent slightly. I could feel her smile. My tongue licked out, sweeping around the taut tight tops of her black stockings. Her skin—white like my white. She tasted of musk and perfume and the scents of flowers. My lips splurged against her thighs.

"Ah, you lick! Like a little doggy you lick," Jenny laughed. After a moment or two she pushed me away with her knees. "It is too soon," she said. I wanted to cry but she would not let me. I was brought to my feet even as the door opened and Jenny rearranged he, dress. My aunt led Caroline in and frowned a little at Jenny, as I thought. The window of the linen room was set high up at the other end from us. The light was morning soft. Caroline wore, as I did, a woollen dress of fine skein.

"You will see to them, Jenny," my aunt said. From our distance I heard my uncle and Katherine enter the house.

There was a tinkling of glasses, laughter. The door closed, leaving the three of us alone.

"Remove your dresses," Jenny said. My hands went to the buttons of mine, but Caroline hesitated. Jenny smacked her and she squealed. "Quickly!" Jenny snapped. We stood naked except for our stockings and boots.

Jenny drew us together, face to face, thighs to thighs. From a drawer she took cords and bound us tightly together —ankles, thighs, waists. We could not move. Our cheeks pressed close. Placing her hands beneath Caroline's bottom she urged us slowly into a corner. I stood with my back to the meeting of the walls. Caroline's breath flowed over my breath.

"Your bodies merge well together," Jenny said, "are your breasts touching fully? Move your breasts. Your nipples must touch."

Yes, I said, yes Jenny. Our nipples were like bell-pushes together. Mine grew and tingled. Caroline's grew. Her toes curled over mine.

"Please, don't," Caroline whispered. I knew that she wasn't speaking to me but in her mind speaking. I moved my lips against her ear. Jenny had gone.

"You like it," I said. I wanted to make her happy. I coaxed her. She had had the cane. Was it nice? "Do you like it?" I asked. I made my voice sound as if we were going on a holiday. If she liked it we would be happy.

"I don't know," Caroline said. Her voice was smudged. Our bellies were silky together. I could feel her slit warm, pulsing. It was nice standing still. I moved my mouth very slowly from her ear to her cheek. I felt her quiver. Had she sucked his cock? I would not ask yet. I would ask later. The tip of my tongue traced the fullness of her lower lip, the Cupid curve. Caroline moved her face away. Her cheeks burned. Our nipples were thorns, entangled.

"Do not!" she choked.

"Jenny will come," I said. Caroline moved her mouth back to mine. The bulbous fullness of her breasts against mine excited me. Our mouths were soft in their seeking. I sought her tongue with my tongue. It retreated, curling in its cave curling. Sipping at her lips I brought it to emerge. The thrill made us quiver. Our nipples moved, implored. My belly pressed in tighter to hers.

The door swung open of a sudden. It was Jenny. She scolded us and said we had been kissing. Working her hand between us she felt our lovemouths, secretive between our thighs. They were moist. Her hand retracted. Her fingers sought our bottoms.

"You must practise—you love one another. Caroline —put your tongue in her mouth."

We swayed. Caroline's tongue was small, urgent, pointed in its flickering. Hidden by our lips our tongues licked. It was a secret. I wanted.

"Open your mouths—let me see your tongues," Jenny commanded. We obeyed.

"Half an hour," Jenny said. She moved to the door and we were alone again. Birds sprinkled their songs among the leaves outside. I was happy. The richness of our bodies flesh to flesh was sweet. Caroline's eyelashes fluttered and tickled against mine. I could feel her belly rippling.

Our tongues like warm snakes worked together. Our thighs trembled. The ridged tops of our stockings rubbed.

Perhaps the door would remain closed forever.

Our minds whispered together like people in caves.

SEVEN

WE would go to meadows, my aunt said. She saw my look of incomprehension. We had been released exactly upon the half hour. Dressed again we sat in the garden and drank champagne and lemonade. It was a reward, Jenny said, because we had not cried or protested when she untied us and made us dress again.

"Meadows—it is a country house your uncle has bought," Aunt Maude explained.

"We may go indoors first?" I asked. I was referring to our own house. My aunt nodded as if surprised at the question.

"Do not tarry—we leave at noon," she told us.

Jenny accompanied us into our house. She was pleased and curious, I believe, to see it again. When I began to assemble clothes she stopped me. "Not that many, Beatrice. Simple dresses only. Be sure to include your riding attire."

I took but one trunk, as did Caroline. A sense of curious excitement seized me. The years rolled back. We were children again preparing for a holiday. We would paddle in the sea or descend from bathing huts whose steps led down into the water and were drawn there by ponies. Ladies were not permitted to expose themselves on the beach, though men could bathe naked so long as they were a far distance from the females.

Unseen by Jenny I took a bottle of liqueur and secreted it. I whispered to Caroline to do the same. She shook her head. Munching a biscuit we waited upon Jenny to conclude her discreet inspection of the house. When she came down she was wearing an ornate hat that Mother had left behind.

"May I have this?" Jenny asked. I do not know why she asked. Perhaps it was to test me. I said no. Not put out, she handed it to the maid and asked her to return it upstairs. "We shall have fun," she said and led us out.

In the roadway stood a large six-seater carriage of a kind not too often seen outside of London or the larger market towns. We ensconced ourselves. The manservant who had accompanied Katherine placed our trunks on top, protected by a guard rail. Our aunt joined us, then my uncle and Katherine. She had changed into a riding outfit with a three-cornered hat—a small one that perched attractively on her hair. She smiled at us with the distant smile of a stranger. The coach, led by four horses, started with a long cracking of a whip. The manservant whose name was Frederick sat up beside the coachman. It was a long and sultry run. I think he enjoyed it little. Katherine toyed with her crop frequently and once or twice teased it playfully about my uncle's thighs. He gained a considerable projection in his breeches in the process, I noticed.

It was a pleasant enough drive, the countryside rolling about us once we had passed through the town. Katherine and Aunt Maude conversed of plays we had not ourselves seen. There was talk of a private theatre at which the actress had evidently appeared.

"We must contrive one," my uncle said, "in the barn perhaps."

"The attic would be splendid, surely," my aunt replied. "It is extremely large," she explained to Katherine. Then she gazed at us as if we were about to speak. I busied myself with counting trees. What did she know of attics? Perhaps she had peered with a telescope from her own to ours. I must tell Father. I would write coded messages, use French words, invisible ink. There would be spies.

Twice on our journey we stopped at inns and took refreshments. "A yard of ale!" my uncle called jovially on entering both, though he had no intention of drinking one. People regarded us curiously. We were strangers. At the second resting place we ate meat pies with thick forks that looked not too clean. Jenny sat with my sister and I ate at a separate table.

"Keep the children quiet, Jenny," my aunt said. We drank ale from pewter mugs. I was constrained. I wanted to sit outside the inn and watch the farm workers pass, wearing their rough smocks. Through the thick panes of leaded glass that was ringed with circles I could see their small images. Father on the water floating. My dress billowing. Fish nibbled at my garters while we embraced. It was said that Nero had boy slaves who swam under water while he was bathing and attended to his penis in the same way. I had read that in a book whose binding was broken. The leathered boards of the book had flopped as Edward's penis had flopped against my thigh.

Jenny took us out while my uncle settled the bill. A

woman bearing a basket and leading a small child passed along the roadway. The child stared and pointed at us.

"Shush! they are from the town," the woman said. She endeavoured to curtsey as she walked. The child wailed and was dragged on. Like the woman its feet were bare.

We journeyed on. The coachman and Frederick had eaten at a table outside. I could hear the coachman belching frequently above the rumbling of the wheels. The coach jolted exceedingly. I dozed. The talking of my aunt, uncle and Katherine was like a murmuring of bees. Jenny had not spoken to them nor been addressed except briefly at the inn.

At last I sat upright as the coach made a sudden turn, the coachman hollering at the horses. There were hedges, stone walls, a rougher road. The coach swayed, throwing us about, as it descended a long slope. Then the house appeared. There were outbuildings. The house was long and made of grey stone. We passed beneath an archway and were in the courtyard.

"Neither of you are to speak," Jenny said. We waited while the others descended and then she bustled us out. A woman wearing a black dress and the cap of a housekeeper stood waiting on the steps. A youth ran past and began to assist the coachman and Frederick in removing the trunks.

"To your rooms," Jenny told us when we entered the hall which was circular.

"May we not see the house—the gardens?" I asked. Jenny stared at me. There was a battle of eyes. "Later," she declared. I sought a softness in her tone and found but a wisp of it. The staircase was circular and broad. The stonework on the surrounding walls provided ledges for the windows. I wanted a white dove to sit in one. Its pink eyes would gaze at me as I passed. I would throw crumbs. It would peck busily. I would wear a white dress with a pink sash.

The sails of Father's ship billowed in the wind. With whom was he talking? Feet trod the boards upon the deck. Men peered at horizons. Beyond them the bronzed women waved and waited.

Our rooms lay together, side by side. We would undress to our stockings and rest, Jenny said. There were pitchers of cool water to drink. We waited while Caroline disrobed and lay down.

"Lie flat on your back and keep your legs apart," Jenny told her. She obeyed. Her blue eyes blinked. Her arms lay at her sides. The soft fern around her pussylips betrayed its gold, its gleaming pink. Closing the door upon her, Jenny turned and kissed me, mouth to mouth. I knew her desire. Our tongues touched. A melting.

"Do you love her?" Jenny asked. I had no need to answer. "We shall have her together," she said. "Do not throw your clothes upon the floor. Be tidy."

I blushed at her silly words. I yearned to be her accomplice, to write messages on trees. She would follow and read them. I would ride on a white horse with my hair flowing. An archer would run beside me.

The room was stark—the stonework not plastered within as I had expected. A large bed stood in the centre of the floor. The foot of it faced the door. The headboard was mirrored with three ovals of glass set in gilt frames. On either side of the bed a cabinet. There was a single wardrobe, heavy in aspect. Its doors were mirrored as was the headboard. A thickpile carpet was the only comfort.

I removed my bonnet and dress slowly, then my chemise and drawers. I was to keep my knee-length boots on, Jenny said, and to keep my stockings straight and taut at all times. My lips must always be slightly parted.

"Why are we here?" I asked. I lay down as Caroline had lain, arms straight at my sides. Jenny nudged my ankles to make my legs part wider. The moisture of the long journey was around and within my cunny. Jenny moved to the end of the bed and gazed at me.

"Erect your nipples," she said. I licked my lips and passed my palms lightly over my breasts, flicking the tips until they rose. The cones pointed from their surrounding circles of crinkled flesh.

"You are to be trained," she told me. "No harm will come to you if you obey." She moved along the bed to the cabinet on my left. A long leaded-glass window with a deep stone sill was also on my left. A vase stood upon it with a single withered flower. Dipping the tips of her fingers into the pitcher of water she sprinkled it upon my breasts. The sudden cold made me start. My nipples quivered and stiffened harder.

What is the purpose of our training, I asked, but the question stayed in my head like a wasp in a jam jar. It buzzed and spun. Jenny turned and gazed down through the window at the meadows beyond.

"Did you want to kiss Katherine?" she asked. "Answer quickly!"

I did not look at her. I knew I must not. I said yes. Questions poured over me. I said yes. I said yes I would like to see her breasts, to kiss her thighs, to tongue her slit. I hated Jenny. She knew it was true.

She had turned away again. She seemed no longer amused by my meanderings. "There will be a reception this evening, Beatrice. I shall instruct you in what to wear. A servant will come for you in an hour. Obey her."

She was gone. A key turned in the lock. I made to rise. Were there cracks in the stone? Watchers? Seekers? My aunt might come. I closed my eyes and walked down corridors of thought. Would Mother return? She had gone with a man to Biarritz, it was said. I remembered his carriage arriving one afterooon, my mother peering through the curtains. He had gazed at us palely.

"I shall not be long," my mother had said. A servant had opened the door for her, gravely. Her footsteps had sounded down the drive, certain, uncertain. A crack of a whip and the coach was gone. Dust rose in the roadway upon its departure. I thought to catch the dust in a jar and watch it swirl forever. It would not do that, Caroline said, when I told her. We had sat quietly until Father had returned that day. He had said nothing of Mother's absence. In the evening I chased a butterfly towards the sun.

I had dozed. A servant was shaking my shoulder. She was the housekeeper I had seen on the steps. I sought my dress, my chemise, my drawers, but they had gone. She tossed a grey cloak down around my feet.

"Come!" She did not call me M'am. I cast the cloak about me. We went up to the floor above and along narrow passageways to a second, smaller staircase. At the foot of it Caroline waited. She was garbed in a cloak as I was. Beneath she wore only her stockings and boots.

"Go!" the woman said. A side door with an iron latch was opened for us by a young servant girl who curtsied. We passed outside onto the stone flags through which grass and weeds sprouted. There were smells of chickens, pigs and hay "Go forward to the stable," the woman said and pointed. My shoulders nudged Caroline's. The knuckles of our hands touched beneath our cloaks. Our feet stumbled over rough grass. The doors of the stable loomed large, yawned open. We were within.

Open shutters allowed rays of sunlight to enter the stable. We passed through the bars of the light to the further wall. There were iron rings, chains. We were made to stand side by side while the woman removed our cloaks. Our arms were raised, spread apart, our wrists secured to rings. The tip of my nose almost touched the timbered wall, as did Caroline's.

Our legs were parted roughly a full three feet so that our stockinged and booted legs were strained. Metallic clicks. Our ankles were secured. Our breathing was tremulous. We dared not to look at one another. The bales of hay about us dreamed of past summers.

There were voices beyond. I felt the woman's return. My head was drawn back. A leather gag was inserted between my lips and tied behind in the nesting of my hair. Caroline's lips would not open to the gag. She received a loud smack. Her yelp gurgled away behind the leather.

"Wash them down," a voice said. Pieces of rough cloth were bound tightly around the tops of our thighs to prevent water trickling down our stockings. There came water, wetness, cold. I jerked. My spine curved. The sponging was insistent. It passed beneath my bottom, cooled my slit. Fingers quested at my lovelips as they urged the sponge. I was forced to strain up on tip-toes. The sponge passed beneath my armpits, in the curls there. It roamed over the hillocks of my breasts. Water tickled me, trickling down my belly. There was laughter as I squirmed. I did not know the voices.

Caroline was attended to next. The sponge trailed longer beneath her quim, I thought. Was I jealous? Her lovemouth pouted no more tightly than my own. A rough towel dried us. Our nipples perked against the wall. The iron rings, the manacles, the bonds about our ankles, clinked.

"Six," a voice said. I sensed a movement new—a soft, insinuating sound as of leather passing across a palm.

Cra-aaaack! Broad width of leather seared across my bottom. *Ah!* I jerked. My belly to the wall I jerked. Cheeks wobbling, tightening, I received another. The sting was sweet, laid full across my buttocks.

A humming whine behind the gag. My own or Caroline's? Father—no! Father would not permit this. Surely his ship would turn, its tall sails straining. Commands. Feet urgent on the deck. My eyes screwed up. The heat flared in my bottom at the next.

"Harder!" I had heard my mother say when Jenny stayed that night.

"Neeynnnng!" Cries strangled in my throat. Flame-searing, the strap took me again. Again. Again. The trees could not see me. The grass did not care. Tears pearled down my cheeks. In my rudeness I squeezed my scorched cheeks tighter.

"Ah, the fullness of her—the thighs, the cheeks. What delicious plumpness," a voice said. Was it Katherine? I heard the cries, unheard, of Caroline. The strap attended to her next. "Let me feel the heat," a voice said. It was the same cultured woman's voice. Palms palmed my wriggling bottom with womanly tenderness. They felt its fullness, the throbbing. Caroline's hip bumped against mine in her squirming. The loud slap-crack of the leather sounded. Fingertips sank insistent in my burning bulge. Cupped, held, I sank my weight upon the palms. My big plum, my pumpkin.

The last crack of the leather.

"Let me feel her," a voice said. Another came whose perfume was as Katherine's. Behind us they stood side by side, controlled our squirmings with their seeking hands. I heard kisses. I could feel tongues. An urgent jerk from Caroline nudged me hard. A small laugh, husky, intimate.

"Not now—not yet," the woman behind me said. Her fingers unclasped as if reluctantly from beneath my bottom. "Is she wet? Tell me," she said, "Ah, give me your tongue!" She had spoken of Caroline. She was wicked. I could not restrain the working of my hips. Long tongues of flame licked through my buttocks still. Baby fingers of warmth moved in my groove. My love-slot pulsed gently. My nipples stiff.

"Leave them—they have been well attended to. What sweet young mares. They can be watered now."

The voice was her voice. I knew her as Katherine now. Our gags were loosened. A tin mug passed between the wall and my mouth and tilted just sufficiently to let water trickle between my lips. I did not want it. I wanted wine. Had the servant unpacked my trunk? She would find my flask of liqueur.

The water had slopped down over Caroline's chin in her blubbering. I could feel it. Globules of water fell and decorated her nipples. Then the doors closed, the big doors in their closing. We were left alone.

I wanted to speak in my speakness. I knew not what to say. Caroline hung her head. Her forehead rested against the wall.

"I love you," I said. The fleshiness of our hips touched. She would not answer me. She made silly, babyish sounds. With my legs wide apart I closed my eyes again and dreamed of the stemming of cocks, the rubicund heads upon the waiting pricks—the nubbing thrust between my open lips. When my bottom was thrust over the end of the rocking horse, the taut cotton had outlined the lips of my honeypot beneath. I had rubbed against the haunches—felt their pleasure.

"It hurts," Caroline whined. I shushed her. We must not be heard. "Squeeze your cheeks," I said. I wanted to touch her bottom, its polished roundness. There were footsteps —a slurring of feet upon the ground, the wisps of hay.

"What have you been doing?" Jenny asked. "Have you been wicked?" She released us. Caroline covered her face. She was ignored. "Put your clothes on—you cannot be seen like that. There are workmen about—rough men," Jenny said.

We donned our cloaks. The tops of my stockings were damp. It was a feeling I liked. The stinging moved in my bottom still, but it was sweeter now. It made me walk differently. My hips swayed more.

"That is good," Jenny said. She could see. She walked behind us. The doors were open again, huge in their hugeness. Two men with pitchforks stood beyond. They touched their caps at our passing. We did not look at them. Their voices were country voices. They breathed of warm milk in stone jars, left overlong on windowsills. Stale cheese—dried scraps of bread. They were rough men. My bottom moved—a silky bulb of heat beneath my cloak.

EIGHT

THERE were crumbs around my mouth. I wiped my lips delicately with my napkin and yawned. After the meal which the servant had brought to my room, I had sipped my liqueur. It had not been taken. The servant who brought the tray was the young girl who had curtsied to us when we had been taken to the stable that morning. Her name was Mary. She was unlearned but pretty. It pleased her to wait upon me. The flush of pleasure lay on her cheeks.

She appeared not surprised to find me naked except for my stockings and boots. On her coming back for the plates, the wine bottle and the glasses, I took her wrist and sat up. I swung my legs over the bed.

"M'am?" she asked. The housekeeper had not called me

M'am. I sensed ranks, classes within classes, initiations. I drew Mary down beside me. "I dares not stay," she said, "they will punish me."

"With the strap?" I asked.

She gazed at the floor. Her feet were shod in neat black boots. Small feet. I would lick her toes perhaps. No. Crumbs of dirt between them. My nose wrinkled with distaste. My hand slid from her wrist and covered her hand. She trembled visibly. Her rosebud mouth was sweet. Such gestures are fatal. They have meaning—like commas, dashes, question marks. I have walked between words. I know the dangers of the spaces between them.

I passed my hand up the nape of her neck and felt her hair. It had not the silkiness of mine, but it was clean. I turned her face, moving my lips over hers. She started like a fawn. I held her. There was a taste of fresh bread in her mouth.

"Tell me," I said.

"There are no answers," a voice said. It was Jenny. She had entered quietly. I neither moved nor sprang up as perhaps she wanted me to. Instead I pressed my mouth again upon the girl's. She trembled in her freshness, a salty dew between her thighs. I felt intimations of boldness. Jenny's hand fell upon my shoulder.

She drew Mary up from my embrace. The girl turned and went, leaving the plates. I made to rise when Jenny fell upon me, spreading my legs by forcing hers between them. The hairs of her pubis were springy to mine through her thin cotton dress. It was a new dress. Small mauve flowers on a blue background. I wanted it.

"There is a wildness in you," Jenny said. Her tongue licked suddenly into my mouth and then withdrew.

"Let me kiss your thighs," I begged. She laughed and

rose, pushing herself up on her forearms slowly so that her breasts bobbed their juicy gourds over mine.

Bereft I lay. Would she seek my tears—kiss the salty droplets? At Christmas Eve I had been carried upstairs with my drawers down. The sea-cry, the wind-cry. Jenny turned to the window and looked down. The darkness now beyond —the mouth of night.

"The stations are all closed—the people have gone. The ships have sailed," she said. I began to cry. She turned and shook me roughly. "The reception will begin soon, Beatrice —get dressed. Stand up!"

Words stuttered in my mouth but knew no seeking beyond. I wanted my nipples to be burnished by her lips. Instead I obeyed quietly as she told me to remove my boots and stockings. In place of the stockings I was to wear tights such as dancers do on the stage. They were flesh-coloured. The burr of my pubic curls showed through. They bulged. A top of the same material was passed over my shoulders. It hugged my waist and hips, fitting so tightly that my nipples protruded into the fine net.

"Longer boots," Jenny said. She pointed to the wardrobe. I padded to it. They had been made ready for me, polished. Sleek-fitting, I drew them on. The heels were narrow and spiked. "Brush your hair—make yourself presentable," Jenny said, "I shall return for you in a minute."

I had not then seen the house except for the back stairs and the entrance hall. There was buzzing of voices as I was made to descend with Caroline—she dressed as I. The grooves between our buttock cheeks showed through the mesh. A piano played. It stopped when we entered. People in formal evening dressed gazed at us and then turned away. Gilt mirrors ranged the walls with paintings between them —one by one around the room. Mary and another girl moved among the visitors with champagne. On sideboards there were canapes in numerous colours. They looked as pretty as flowers on their silver trays.

The piano played again. Mozart, I thought. Men looked at my breasts and buttocks. Their eyes fanned Caroline's curves. The high heels made us walked awkwardly, stiffly. The cheeks of our bottoms rolled.

To the one blank wall farthest from the doors Jenny led us, a hand on each of our elbows. There were clamps, chains, bands of leather.

Caroline first. Her legs were splayed, her ankles fastened. Her arms above her head.

"Hang your head back—let your bottom protrude!" Jenny snapped at her. I wanted to be blindfolded. I knew it was good to be so. Black velvet bands swathed our eyes. In darkness we stood, our shoulders touching warm. The manacles were tight.

I had seen my uncle. He watched upon our obedience. I heard his voice. There was silence in the room. The last chords of the piano tinkled and were gone. A wink of fishes' tails and gone.

Caroline first. I heard the intake of her breath as he passed his hands up the backs of her thighs and squeezed her bottom cheeks. "My doves," he breathed. He placed a broad, warm palm on each of our bottoms. People clapped. The room stirred again, came alive.

We were left. Knuckles slyly nudged our bottoms from time to time. Were we forbidden? Female fingers touched more delicately. With the protrusion of our bottoms and the splaying of our legs, our slits were at pillage. Mine wettened into the mesh of the tights as slender fingers quested and sought the lips. And found. I tried not to wriggle my hips.

Champagne was passed between our lips from goblets unseen. I absorbed mine greedily. I could hear Caroline's tongue lapping. There was dancing. I heard the feet. The plaintive cry of an oboe accompanying the piano. If it were a girl playing I would know her by her slimness, her tight small mouth that only an oboe reed would enter. Her face would be oval and pale, her breasts light and springy. She would speak little. Her words would be dried corn, her days spent in quiet rooms. At the high notes I envisaged her on a bed in a white cell. She would not struggle. Her stockings would be white, her thighs slender.

Laid on her back, she would breathe slowly, quietly, fitfully through her nose. Her dress would be raised. Knees would kneel on the bed between her legs. Her knees would falter, stir and bend. Her bottom would be small and tight. Hands would cup and lift. She would wear white gloves of kid. I had almost forgotten the gloves. They would be decorated with small pearl buttons spaced half an inch apart.

No words. Her mouth would be dry. A small dry mouth. Her cunny would be dry. A small dry cunny. A tongue would moisten it—her fingers would clench. She would close her eyes. Her eyelashes would have the colour of straw.

Her knees would be held. The knob-glow of a penis three times the girth of her oboe would probe her slit. A small cry. A quavering. In her dryness. Entering, deep-entering it would enter. Lodged. Held full within. The tightness there. In rhythmic movement it would move, the lips expanding around the stem.

Silently he would work, upheld on forearms bared, gazing down upon the pallor of her face.

Her buttocks would twitch and tighten. A crow would alight at the window. Pecking at stone it would be gone.

The penis moving, stiff. A small bubble of sound from her lips, suppressed. The tightening of her buttocks would compress the sealskin walls that gripped him. In his oozing he would groan. Deep in him he would groan. His face would bend. His lips would move over her dry eyelids.

She would not stir. There were no words to speak for her. In the white cell of her room a rag doll would smile and loll against the wall. Through her nostrils now her breath would hiss. Music scores would dance through her mind. The oboe of flesh would play in her.

"*Pmmffff!*" Her breath explodes, mouth opens. He ravages her mouth, she struggles, squirms. His loins flash faster. Faint velvet squelch between their loins. Her cuntlips grip like a clam. He clamps her bottom, draws the cheeks apart. Mutinous still, her tongue retreats, unseeking to his seeking.

The sperm boils. In the itching stem the lava rises. The bed rocks. Music of lust. There is dryness here in the love-lust dry. The curtains falter and wave. Her bottom is lifted, back arched. His pestle pounds.

She receives. The squirting she receives—the long thin jets. Spatter-tingling of sperm. Their breath hush-rushes. Her arms lie limp. Long-leaping strands of wet. The oozy. Last jet of come. The dribbling. The last tremors. Bellies warm. A weakness, falling. The strong loins of his urging are paper now. Strengthless he lies, then moves from her.

Her face is pallid. She awaits his going and rises. Her dress is straightened. A vague fussing of hair. Quiet as a wraith she descends.

"You will have tea now, dear? You have had your lesson?" she is asked. She nods. Her knees tremble. A warm trickling between her thighs. The oboe, yes. The tall ship sailing.

I emerged from my dreams. We were loosed and turned about, our bonds replaced. My bottom bulbed to the wall. I waited.

NINE

THERE was quiet again. The music ceased again. I had not liked it. Its feebleness irritated.

The Lady Arabella was announced. I turned my head, though I could not see.

"Let her enter and be brought here," I heard my uncle say. There was a sound as if of a heavy table moving. Jenny's hands moved about my face. I knew the scent and taste of them. Her fingertip bobbled over my lower lip. The blindfold slipped down an inch beneath my eyes.

"Look," Jenny said. I saw the woman enter. Her coiffure was exquisite. A diamond choker, a swan neck. Her curves were elegant beneath a swathing white gown of satin flecked with red. The collar of her gown was raised slightly at the back, as one sees it in portraits of the Elizabethans.

She wore a look of coldness and distance. Her lips were full, her nose long and straight. Her eyelids were shadowed in imitation of the early Egyptians.

She made to step back as my uncle reached her. Her fingers were a glitterbed of jewels. Behind her entered a man of military look, impeccable in a black jacket and white trousers, as was the evening fashion then. I judged the years between them. She was the younger.

"Not here. It is unseemly," she said.

Jenny covered my eyes. Did she then uncover Caroline's? I heard not a sound beside me.

"No," the woman said in answer to some muttered remark. There was movement past me. I felt it. As the air moves I felt. Hands touched my thighs, caressed. A finger traced the lips of my quim which pressed its outlines through the fine mesh of the tights. It was removed quickly, as if by another. I heard the jangling of bracelets.

"Not here," the woman said again. I felt her as if surrounded, jostled. They would not dare to jostle, but they had touched me. Was I an exhibit?

"B . . . Beatrice. . . ." A croaking whisper from my sister. I ignored her. I heard her squeal. She always squeals. She was being fingered. Her bonds jangled. The girl with the oboe would be tight. The sperm would squirt in her thinly. Would she feel it?

Jenny favoured me. Once more my blindfold slipped. The chandeliers danced their crystal diamonds. The Lady Arabella was moving forward. As if through water she moved. An older woman moved beside her, a hand cupping her elbow. The older woman wore a purple dress. Her vulgarity was obvious.

"Arabella, my sweet, you will come to dinner tomorrow night? The Sandhursts are coming." Her voice cooed.

"I do not know. Perhaps, yes. I must look in my diary, of course."

Arabella's look was constrained, her lips set. Behind her, as I felt, the man who had escorted her in was nudging her bottom. It was of an ample size, though not too large by comparison with her stately curves. Her face turned to her escort as if pleading. He shook his head. I saw the table then. It had indeed been pushed forward. Upon its nearest edge was a large velvet cushion. Her long legs appeared to stiffen as she approached it. Her footsteps dragged. Her shoes were silver as I saw from the occasional peeping of her toes beneath the hem of her gown.

Jenny covered my eyes again. I had not looked at Caroline. Her veins throbbed in mine. Her lips were my lips. We had been bound together naked. I had sipped her saliva.

There were murmurings, whispers, protestations, retreats. The doors to the morning room opened and closed, re-opened and closed again.

"It is private," I heard my aunt say to others. The room was stiller. I heard a cry as from Arabella.

"Lift her gown fully," a voice said, "hold her arms."

"Not here. . . ." She seemed unable to say anything else. Not here, not here, not here, not here. A rustling sound. Slight creak of wood. A gasp. Plaintive.

"Remove her drawers."

"She was unseemly? Is she not betrothed to him?" It was my aunt's voice. To whom she spoke I knew not. I guessed it to be the escort. His voice was dry and thin.

"Improper," he replied. The word fell like the closing of a book. "Take them right off. Do not let her kick," he said.

"No! not the birch!" A wail from Arabella. The modulations of my aunt's voice and the military gentleman's amused me. They were tonally flat—courteous. Would he have her bound, my aunt asked. It was not necessary, he said, but her wrists should be held.

I envisaged her bent over the table, the globe of her bottom gleaming. Her garters would be of white satin, flecked with red. The deep of her groove—the inrolling. Her breathing came to me, filtering its small waiting sobs. The dry rustling sound of a birch. I had never yet tasted the twigs. It was said that they should be softened first.

"Not bound," my aunt said. Her voice sounded almost regretful. "Hilda—you will hold her wrists tight. Stretch her arms out."

"Noooooo!"

The long, sweet aristocratic cry came as the first swishing came. It sounded not as violently as I thought. I wanted to see. My mind groped, grappled for Jenny. Perhaps she had been sent with others to the morning room. Beside me Caroline uttered a small whimper. Did she fear the birch? She would not receive it. I would protect her. I ran through tunnels calling Father's name. Edward had used his stepmother's first name. She had permitted it. He had lain upon her.

"Na! Naaaaah!" A further cry. Her sobbing rose like violins. A creaking of table. Beneath her raised gown, her underskirt, her chemise, the velvet cushion would press beneath her belly. There was comfort. I comforted myself with the comfort.

The sounds went on. The birch swished gently but firmly as it seemed to me. First across one cheek then the other, no doubt. The bouncy hemispheres would redden and squirm. Streaks of heat. Was it like the strap? I did not like the stable. Did I like it?

"Ask her now," the man's voice came. There was whispering—a quavering cry. A negation. Refusal. "Three more," he said, "her drawers were down when I caught them together."

My aunt tutted. The small dots of her tutting impinged across the sobs, the swishings. They flew like small birds across the room.

"Whaaah! No-ooooh! Wha-aaaaah!" Arabella sobbed. I felt her sobs in my throat, globules of anguish swelling. They contracted, slithered down. There was quiet. Her tears would shine upon the polished wood of the table.

"Ask her again." The same voice, impassive, quiet. The sobs were unending.

"Have you before?" my aunt asked. It was her garden voice, clear and enquiring. The lilt of a question mark that could not fail to invite.

"Twice—but she resists. What does she say?" He asked as if to another.

"I cannot hear. Arabella, you must speak, my dear, or take the birch again." It was undoubtedly the voice of the woman holding her wrists. Who held the birch?

"I c . . . c . . . cannot. No—yes—oh do not. Do not let him!"

I saw nods. Through my blindfold I saw nods. I envisaged. There was a shuffling. Wrists tighter held. A jerk of hips. The arrogant bottom out-thrust, burning.

"No! not there! *Ah!* it is too big! Not *there!"*

The floor drummed in my dreams. His penis extended, fleshpole, thickpole, entering. Smack-slap of flesh. The chandeliers glittering with their hundred candles.

Her sobs died, died with their heaving groans. "N . . . n . . . n . . . n . . ." she stuttered from moment to moment. At every inward thrust the table creaked. Was she still being held? I needed voices, descriptions.

"Work your bottom, Arabella! Thrust to him!"

My aunt spoke. Their breathings flooded the room. A

gulping gasp. A last sob. Silence. "Have her dress," my aunt said at last. "Hilda—see to her hair, bathe her face, she has been good. Have you not been good, Arabella?" A mumbling. Kissing. "So good," my aunt said. Bodies moved, moved past us and were gone. The doors to the morning room were re-opened. A flooding of people, a flurry, voices. Enquiries. My aunt would not answer. The deeper voice of my uncle said occasionally, "I do not know."

My limbs ached, yet I was proud in my aching that I had not struggled. I was free in my proudness, my pride. We could speak but we had not spoken. Our minds whispered. We were wicked.

A chink of light. Our blindfolds were removed. Caroline blinked more than I. She had not seen before. People stared at us more strangely now. They were of all ages. Eyes glowed at the bobbing of our breasts.

"You must go to bed. A servant will bring you supper," Jenny said.

I moved carefully, cautiously—wanting to be touched, not wanting to be touched. My hips swayed. I thought of Arabella.

As we reached the bottom of the stairs she began to descend. We waited. I wanted to be masked. Accompanying her was the older woman in purple. I knew then that it was she who had held her wrists. Their eyes passed across us unseeing.

"And there will be a garden party—for the church, you know," the woman in purple said.

Arabella's eyes were clear, her voice soft and beautifully modulated.

"Of course—I should love to come," she replied. They entered the drawing room together as we went up.

"Did you see?" Caroline asked me the next morning.

"There was nothing to see. People were making noises," I replied. I wanted her to sense that I was more innocent than she.

"Uncle felt my breasts," she said.

She looked pleased.

TEN

I LIKE the mornings, the bright mornings, the sun-hazed mornings.

It was so when we sat in the breakfast room that morning, Caroline and I. The chairs had been taken away save for hers and mine.

"You will breakfast alone in future," our aunt said. "Eat slowly, chew slowly. Have you bathed?" We nodded. Jenny passed the door and looked in at us. Her face held the expression of a sheet of paper. There was a riding crop in her hand. It smacked a small smacking sound against her thigh.

The drawing room had looked imacculate as we passed—its doors wide open, announcing innocence. The walls against which we had been bound were covered with mirrors, paintings. Perhaps we had dreamed the night.

There would be riding, Aunt Maude said. We were not to change. Our summer dresses would suffice. Katherine passed the window, walking on the flagstones at the edge of the lawn. She wore a long white dress that trailed on the ground. The neck was low and frilled. The melons of her breasts showed. Her straw hat was broadbrimmed. There were tiny flowers painted around the band. She carried a white parasol. Her servant walked behind her in a grey uniform.

When we had eaten Jenny came again to the door and beckoned us. We followed her through the grounds and beyond the fence into the meadow. Frederick stood waiting, holding the reins of two fine chestnut horses. They were gifts to us, Jenny said. The leather of the new saddles was covered in blue velvet.

We were told to mount. The servant looked away. He studied the elms on the high rise of the ground in the distance.

"Swing your legs over the saddles. You will ride as men ride. No side-saddle," Jenny told us. The breeze lifted my skirt, showing my bottom. We wore no drawers. I exposed my bush. Frederick had turned to hold the reins of both horses. The stallions stood like statues. The velvet was soft and warm between my thighs. The lips of my pussy spread upon it.

Jericho.

Jenny said we were to ride around her in a tight circle, I clockwise, Caroline counter-clockwise. The servant turned my horse. I faced the house. It looked small and distant. A doll's house. When we returned and entered it we would become tiny.

Jenny clapped her hands and we began. The movement

of the velvet beneath me made my lips part with pleasure. Caroline's face was flushed as she passed me, the flanks of our steeds almost brushing. Our hair rose and flowed outwards in the breeze. We kept our backs straight as we had been taught. Father could not have reached up so high to smack me.

"Straighten your legs—lift your bottoms—high!" Jenny called. She stood in the middle of the circle we made. The breeze lifted our skirts, exposing us. The hems of our skirts curled and flowed about our waists. The sky spun about me.

"Higher!" Jenny commanded. Our knees straightened. Frederick had gone. I was pleased. In profile the pale moon of Caroline's bottom flashed past me. I heard her squeal, a long thin squeal as the crop caught her, light and stinging across her out-thrust cheeks. And then mine! The breath whistled from my throat. I kept my head back. In the far distance near the house two figures were watching. My uncle was watching. Katherine's head lay on his shoulder, her parasol twirling.

Again the crop. It skimmed my naked bottom cheeks, not cutting but skimming as if it were skittering across the face of a balloon. Who had taught her that? It stung, lifting me up on to my toes in the stirrups. I leaned forward, clutching at the horse's mane, breathing my whistling cries to the far-deep empty sky.

At the twelfth stroke of the crop upon each of us, Jenny raised her hand. We slowed, we cantered, we reined in. Panting we fell forward, exposing our burning bottoms to the air. The breeze was cool across our pumpkins hot.

"Dismount!" Jenny called. Frederick the servant was returning. He carried things. "Stable them!" Jenny ordered him. She referred I thought to the horses, but he ignored them. My bottom tightened as he approached. The ground would receive me—surely it would receive me. I would bury myself in the longer grass and hide until I was called in to tea. I would be fifteen again.

The leather collar bands that I now saw in the servant's hands were broad and thick, studded with steel points on the outer surfaces. My eyes said no but he did not look. I wrote a question silently on my lips as I used to do with father in the attic. The servant could not read. He fastened the first collar around my neck. A chain ran down my back. The tip of it settled in the outcurving of my buttocks. From behind me then where Caroline stood I heard a small cry.

"No, Caroline, be still!" Jenny hissed. "Walk forward to the barn now!"

Behind us the servant held the chains, one in each hand like reins. We stumbled over the grass, the rough hillocks.

"Why?" Caroline asked. It was only to herself that she spoke, but Jenny answered her. She walked beside us, ushering our steps.

"Love is firmness, Caroline. You are the privileged ones. Halt!"

We had neared the stable doors. They were open. The darkness within yawned upon the meadow, eating the air that came near it. Katherine was there. She closed her parasol and leaned it against one of the doors.

"Leave this—I will see to them," she told Jenny.

"Yes, Madame," Jenny answered. Was she not queen? Who was queen? The chains snaked against our backs, urging us forward. And within. In the flushing of Caroline's cheeks I could feel my flushing.

"Over there," Katherine said and pointed. There were two stalls—too narrow for horses. The dividing wall between them was but a foot high. I saw the chains again, the wall rings. Caroline wilted and would have stepped back. She was prodded forward. The manacles, ankle rings and chains all were secured. We stood side by side, the low wall between us. I wanted the back of my hand to touch Caroline's hand, but it could not.

"Their dresses, you fool—raise their skirts," Katherine said. I felt Frederick's hands. They were strong but delicate. Not touching my legs or bottom he bared me to my waist. Caroline quivered and bit her lip as he repeated the action with her.

"Wash their flanks," Katherine said.

I heard a clink of bucket. The sponge attended to us both. Water trickled over our buttocks and thighs. It ran down into the tops of my stockings and lay in rills around the tight rims. Patted roughly, we were dried.

"They are fair mounts. What do you think, Frederick?"

"Yes, Madame."

His voice was stiff, expressionless. I relaxed my bottom, feeling its glow—the aftermath of the cropping. The outcurving cheeks above my dampy thighs were roseate. I could see them in my mind. I wished I could see Katherine now in her white dress, but my back was held to her. She is very beautiful. Her dark hair flows down over her shoulders.

"Display, Frederick!"

Her voice was curt. She waited. I could hear her waiting, the sound of her waiting, like a bell that has stopped tolling and waits for the rope to be pulled again.

"Madame?"

His voice was a croak. Was he afraid? I felt not afraid. The day lay upon me, soft of the morning. My flesh bloomed. The damp upon my flesh was warm with my flesh. The tops of my stockings chilled. Caroline breathed through her nose. There were noises, shufflings, small metal noises, cloth noises.

Cloth makes noises like fog.

Display? What was display?

"Turn them!" I heard Katherine say. Ah, it was strange. He held his loins back as he obeyed so that the wavering crest of his pintle-pestle would not touch us. It was long and thick. I like long and thick now. The chains rattled. We were turned. I saw through the barn doors as through a huge eye. The world outside disenchanted me. There was an emptiness. Katherine sat on a bale, her legs crossed. Her skirts were drawn up to show her knees. She smiled at me a light smile, a wisp of a smile. Caroline's face was scarlet. The servant was naked. His balls were big. His penis was a horn of plenty.

We stood side by side still—children waiting to be called to the front of the class. For punishment or to be given prizes? Frederick's body was slender, muscular.

"Come!" Katherine said to him. He turned and moved to her. His back was to us, but he did not look at her. I could feel he did not. His glance was high. Above her head. In homage high. There was a trestle close—two pairs of legs shaped in a narrow V with a bar across. He moved to the front of it and stopped. His back touched the bar. Then he bent—a backward bend—so that his spine arched over the bar, his palms flat on the floor beyond. His penis stuck straight up.

Katherine moved her long wide skirt with an elegant gesture and slipped down off the bale. She came to us. We had kept our legs apart. She was pleased.

"Caroline will lie with her face between my thighs tonight, Beatrice. I shall wear black stockings—pearls around my neck. My thighs will clench her ears. Will you see? Do you wish to see?"

My eyes pleaded. She laughed. She squeezed my chin until my lips parted. "You can see his cock," she breathed. Her tongue snaked within my mouth. I tasted the breath of her, warm and sweet as Benedictine. She twirled her tongue, then moved to Caroline.

"Put your tongue in my mouth—*Caroline!*"

Oh, the fool—she should have obeyed immediately. Katherine slapped her face. The tip of Frederick's prick quivered.

"I shall commence exercising you soon, Caroline. Do you understand?"

"No." My sister's voice was small as if she were hiding behind a pew in church.

"You say, 'No, Madame.'"

"No, Madame."

Caroline can be dutiful. I like her body. It curves so sweetly. Her breasts and bottom are plentiful.

"You will learn," Katherine said. Then Jenny entered. It was a play—a private play, I felt. She stood in the doorway, hands on hips, observing us. Was she jealous? When Katherine turned, Jenny's hands dropped immediately to her sides. There were no words yet. It was a mime.

"Let him rise," Katherine commanded. Jenny smiled. She walked forward and flicked her crop against his straining tool. He groaned in his rising. His eyes were haggard.

"You may choose," Katherine told her. Jenny tossed her head. She looked from one to the other of us. She strode—strode to Caroline and pulled her forward.

"Please no," Caroline said. Her feet skittered, dragged. Her free hand pleaded to the air. The chaffeur had turned to face her. He had tucked our dresses up sufficiently tightly for them to remain so. I wanted to kiss Caroline's bottom. The cheeks are firm and plump. Her pubis pouts.

"Bend her over the trestle," Katherine said.

Caroline shrieked. Jenny had hold of the chain from her neckband and pulled it tight, forcing her over. Caroline's shriek dropped like a fallen handkerchief and lay there, crumpled and used. Her back was bent until she was forced to place her palms on the floor. Her bottom mounded. The sweet fig of her slit showed.

The servant waited. His erection remained as stiff as ever. There was excitement.

"Dip!" Katherine said.

There were new words. I was learning them. Display—dip. His eyes burned. Caroline's hips were high. He took them, gripped them. Rebelliously she endeavoured to twist them but he held her. His lips moved. I wanted words to come—a revelation—but no words came. His loins arched. The crest of his penis touched, probed.

"Caroline! Do not move or speak or you will be whipped!" Katherine said.

She stood observing, as one observes. It was so in the drawing room the night before when my aunt watched the waiting penis enter between the cheeks of Arabella's bottom. I could see now only the servant's haunches, his balls hanging below. Caroline bubbled a moan. Was it speech? His shaft entered—slow, but slow—the petal lips parting to receive it. The straining veins, the purplish head, the foreskin stretched.

Caroline's head jerked up and then was pulled back down by the tensioning of the chain in Jenny's grip.

"*No,* Caroline!" Jenny said softly.

Four inches, five. Caroline's mouth opened. Perhaps she had not, as I thought, sucked upon the penis. Her love-mouth gripped. The ring of truth. Cries gurgled from her lips. Six inches, seven. The fit was tight. I saw her buttocks squeeze, relax. His hands moved to the fronts of her thighs, suavely gripping them. A burr of stocking tops to his palms.

"*No-ooooh!*"

A soft, faint whimper. *In!* Ensconced. Buried to the hilt, his balls hung beneath her bottom.

A second ticked. Two. Three.

"*Out!*" Katherine snapped.

Gleaming, his shaft emerged. I saw his face in profile, the lines etched as by Durer. She jerked her head. He moved towards his clothes. Caroline blubbered softly, her hips wriggled as if she still contained him. Jenny drew her up by the chain. Caroline's eyes floated with tears. Her face suffused.

In the house—not until in the house—were our neck halters removed. We stood in the morning room. We waited. Katherine moved to Caroline and stroked her cheek.

"Are you learning?" she asked. There was summer in her voice.

"Madame?"

Caroline's voice was blank, soft as the sponge that had laved us. Katherine shook her head. "It does not matter," she said. We shared secrets, but I knew not what they were. The secret between Caroline's thighs tingled. I could feel its tingling like a buzzing on my lips. Caroline was wicked. I felt certain that she was. Her containment had been too great. She should have cried. Would I have cried? Kathy turned away.

"You know I will whip you if you do not tell me, Caroline."

Caroline's lips moved, burbled, hummed. "M . . . m . . . m . . ." Her thighs trembled. Kathy turned back to her.

"That is better," she smiled, "you are naughty, Caroline, you know you are. I have to train you. Edward is trained. Do you not think he is well trained?"

Caroline bent her head. She was alone. Each of us alone except when we are kissing, touching. Sometimes when I am being touched I am alone. There was a small cloud around her lips, pretty lips. It said yes. Katherine was pleased again. Aunt Maude entered. There was movement. Unspeaking she took my arm and led me out.

Upstairs in my room she removed my dress. I saw the bed and it was not my bed, not the bed I had slept in. The headboard was different. Wrist clamps hung from the headboard. She made me lie down. She straightened my stockings and drew my legs apart. I waited for my ankles to be secured. I was passive. She drew my arms above my head and fastened the wrist straps. Her face bent over mine.

"It is for your good, Caroline. Are you happy?"

I said yes. I wanted to please her. Proud in my bonds I lay. My belly made a slight curve.

"Perhaps," she answered. It was a strange word. "You will grow happy. Edward was weak for you, was he not?"

I nodded. The morning light grew and bloomed over my body. I had fine breasts, good haunches, a slender waist, Aunt Maude said. Was Jenny nice to me, she asked. I thought yes, no. I wanted to be kissed. I parted my lips as Jenny had told me to. I was not sure, Aunt Maude said. I would be sure soon. She bent over and kissed me and laid her fingers on the innerness of my nearest thigh. Her mouth was warm and full.

"Flick your tongue a little, Beatrice. Quick little flicks with half your tongue."

She was teaching me. Our mouths fused together. Her forefinger brushed my button—too lightly. My hips bucked. My aunt stopped kissing me and smiled. She sat up. Regarding me, she unbuttoned her dress and laid it back from her shoulders. Her breasts were heavy gourds, the nipples dark brown and thick. Brown in their darkness brown. The gourds loomed over my face, brushed my chin, my nose. My aunt purred a purring sound. Her breasts swung like bells across my mouth. The nipples grew and teased between my lips. I wanted to bite.

Katherine entered. She waited and my aunt rose.

"He has not whipped her yet?" Katherine asked. Aunt Maude shook her head.

"Soon, perhaps."

"Yes," Katherine said. She removed her dress, the filmy folds. Her stockings were silver, banded by black garters of ruched silk. Her drawers were of black satin, small, such as a ballet dancer wears. Her breasts jiggled free. She sat at the dressing table beside my bed. Aunt Maude stripped off her own dress and stood at Katherine's back, brushing her hair. They smiled at one another in the mirror. The smile would stay there for a moment like the impress of my lips when I used to kiss myself after father had spanked me.

Katherine rose. My aunt looked superb in her stockings, bootees, a waspie corset, frilled knickers. They exchanged sentences with their eyes as if they were posting small, personal notes. My aunt nodded. Katherine mounted the bed over me at my shoulders, facing my feet. The moon of her bottom loomed over my face.

"Her legs," she said.

The board of the bed to which my ankles were now tethered and spread moved forward, making my knees bend. It was an ingenious device, as I later discovered. The upright board was fixed to the legs which rested on heavy castors. Being slightly wider than the bed itself, the legs and the board were able to be moved at will. My knees were bent up, splayed. The globe of Katherine's knickered bottom brushed the tip of my nose. It descended. In a darkness of bliss it squashed upon my mouth, my eyes, my face.

I tasted her.

"Do not move your lips, Beatrice—it is forbidden!"

I could not breathe. The fleshweight of her hemispheres was upon me. The impress of the lips of her slit in their silken net were upon my mouth. Her bottom bloomed its bigness over me. I panted.

Her bottom moved, ground over my face. It lifted but an inch. I gulped in air. Smothered again, I grunted, gasped. Aunt Maude had a feather. The tip of it, the tickling tip of it, passed upwards in my cunny. I gurgled, choked. The feather twirled, inserted and withdrew. Air whistled through my nostrils and was squashed again. My loins shifted, jerked.

The agony of ecstasy was intense at the feather's touching. A wisping of wickedness, it passed around my clit, tickling and burning. My bottom thumped. The bed creaked. The sides of my face were gripped tight between Katherine's silken thighs. Long tendrils of desire urged their desire within my cunny. My bottom lifted, pleading, in my smothering. Musk, perfume, acrid sweetness—I knew them all.

Let me be loved, in my desiring.

No—Katherine swung off me. Her panties were wet. Sweat glistened on my brow, my cheeks. My loins itched, stung. My mouth was wet with her. I closed my eyes and whispered with Caroline behind a pew. We wore candy-striped blouses, pretty bonnets. We chewed bonbons. I wanted one.

They turned me quickly, unloosing the shackles swiftly. Once on my belly the bonds were refastened. The board at the foot of the bed pressed farther up, forcing my knees up almost to my breasts. The cleft of my pumpkin was exposed.

Something nosed between my cheeks. A velvet touch, a thin dildo of leather swathed in a velvet sheath. The oiled nose of it probed my rose, the tight puckering of my secret mouth, the O of my anus.

"N . . . n . . . n . . . n. . . ." I choked. It penetrated sleekly, entered. My mouth mouthed in my pillow. In the heat of it, the ice of it, I felt it, slender, long, like Edward's penis. Edward had never attempted my bottom. He did not know it had been smacked.

"Oooooh!"

One should not cry out. Should one cry out? I am quieter now. I accept. I am given, loved, I submit. In my moods. It was different then. My bottom mouth gripped it in a grip of treachery—the sleek black velvet of my velvet love. The pointed nose oozed in and twirled. My bottom was riven. In the wild twisting of my face and hips I saw Katherine's legs. Thighs of ivory splendour. Rotating, it withdrew. I was opened. I bit my pillow. The stinging sweetness tremored in my loins. The oil which had been smoothed upon it made it slippery. I grimaced, cried. Katherine laughed.

"Enough—it is enough. How sweetly she sobs—how her bottom bulges to it."

"It was so when she was spanked. She should be whipped now," my aunt said. A faint succulent *plop* and it deserted me. I was hollow, empty. I needed. My O was a bigger O. I dived beneath sandcastles of shame. My toes wriggled. *Foutre.*

Was Father's ship sailing back? It would beach at Eastbourne. People on the beach would run screaming, the pebbles sliding beneath their feet. My father with a cutlass would descend.

They released me. The board moved back. My legs straightened. My wrists and ankles were freed. I sank down, curling up. I would become a hedgehog. Gypsies would catch me.

"Shall we go out now, Beatrice?"

It was Katherine's voice. I turned. She was putting on her dress. My aunt was putting on her own dress. She buttoned it with the air of someone who had had it accidentally removed, or by a doctor perhaps. I hid my eyes.

"Yes," I said. I felt shy. Katherine clapped her hands with pleasure. She reached down and pulled me up.

"Come—get dressed you silly girl. How old are you?"

"Twenty-five," I said. I had said that to father. They all knew. Why did they ask? Aunt Maude scolded me to brush my hair.

"Don't be a naughty girl, Beatrice," she said.

ELEVEN

FACING the open gates my uncle sat holding the reins of the horses. The cab was the same that we had arrived in.

Caroline and I wore straw boaters, plain high-necked white blouses and long black skirts. Our hair was drawn back with ribbons. My aunt and Katherine entered with us.

"Keep your hands still," my aunt said. There was a jerk and the carriage started up the slope. It bumped exceedingly again. At the top we turned right—in the opposite direction to which we had come—and proceeded along the lanes. A few yokels moved aside at our coming, but otherwise no other carriage passed us.

Aunt Maude and Katherine toyed with their gloves and spoke of balls, receptions, dances. I envied their pleasures.

My face was demure. I wanted to ask where we were going but I knew it was forbidden. After some six miles we reached a place that was too small for a town and yet too large to be a village.

Over the cobbles of the streets we rattled until we came to a house facing a pond and a green. Two children ran playing with hoops over the grass. The house was of stone, the windows small. It was set amid a walled garden.

"Shall they come in?" Katherine asked. My aunt nodded. They descended first. My uncle helped us down. His expression was one of great seriousness. He was dressed formally in top hat, grey jacket, waistcoat and black trousers.

He led us forward towards the gate to the drive of the house as if we were approaching for a family portrait to be taken. The door was black, inset with frosted glass. The knocker was of brass in the semblance of a lion's head. There was a bell which my uncle pulled. It tinkled with broken notes somewhere within. Almost immediately a servant maid answered. She curtsied at the sight of my uncle and aunt.

My uncle presented his card as we entered the hall. The maid took it upon a small silver tray and vanished. In but a moment she returned and ushered us within a drawing room where a middle-aged couple sat in highbacked chairs. They rose as one. Not having the advantage of facing the sun, the room had a certain gloom.

I waited to be introduced. Instead, Katherine pointed to a small love-seat in one corner. "Sit there," she said. We threaded our way through the furniture and sat like doves, side by side, our hands in our laps.

Port was dispensed. We each received a glass. To my astonishment and amid the blushes of Caroline my aunt spoke of us to the lady she addressed as Ruby. She gave our ages and certain details of our training. We sat mute. Only our Christain names were given.

"They are most certainly quiet and well-behaved," the lady said. She turned her gaze upon us and appraised us. We kept our eyes lowered—Caroline out of shyness and confusion, I out of discernment. I felt it would please her. It did. The gentleman displayed a greater interest in us. Leaning forward in his chair he spoke in a low voice to my aunt. Twice she nodded then he rose. He approached us, fiddling with his watch chain. We stirred not.

"Do not move," Katherine said quietly to us, "Look up!"

We raised our eyes. He was a stocky man in his prime. Caroline gave a little jump as he bent down and placed his hands upon her blouse, cupping her breasts. I could feel their warmth and weight as on my own hands. He attended next to my own, running the balls of his thumbs about my nipples. They stirred and pointed into the cotton of my blouse. His hands trembled exceedingly. The projection in his breeches was one of considerable menace.

He returned to his seat. His breathing sounded laboured. Katherine's eyes remarked his condition, I know. His wife laid her hand upon his when he took his chair again beside her. Her glance came to us again.

"May we take them upstairs?" she asked.

My aunt inclined her head. "I regret . . ." she said. Her voice was formal as if she were writing the words on parchment. "We should see Amanda, perhaps."

There was a nodding. The servant was summoned. Miss Amanda would be asked to come down, she was told. We waited. The clock upon the mantlepiece threw tiny arrows of sound into the carpet. My nipples grew turgid again and softened. Footsteps. The door opened. A young lady of about twenty-three years appeared. She was dressed in simple attire: a blue dress that clothed her form admirably.

A tasselled cord of blue velvet drew the material in at her waist. She was slender. Her legs were long. Her high breasts made themselves appealingly visible through the material. Her dark hair was swept back behind her ear. A pearl necklace and matching earrings adorned her. Her eyes were large and faintly wondering. Her mouth had a petulant look.

There were introductions from which my sister and I were again excluded. Amanda looked towards us. We avoided her glance as if by inverted politeness. Amid the chairs she stood like a hunted fawn.

"I do not want to go," she said. Her voice was shrunken, distant. Katherine's eyes absorbed the delicate outcurving of her bottom.

"It will take but a month, perhaps less," my aunt said. She spoke as if Amanda were not present. The seance it seemed was then at end. There was a rising as if of marionettes.

"Take your cloak," the lady said to Amanda who had laid small white teeth into her lower lip.

"But if I promise . . ." Amanda began.

"It is a nonsense—she will not even be spanked," the lady said, addressing my aunt. In the same moment Katherine took Amanda's wrist. "Come!" she said sharply. We knew that the word was addressed to ourselves as well. A bustling, a rustling, an opening and closing of doors and we were gone. The carriage kicked up a fine dust with its departure. The children with the hoops stared after us. Amanda sat pale and quiet between Caroline and I.

"Amanda—you must not be dismayed, we shall treat you well," my aunt said, "There will be strawberries and cream for tea." Caroline and I smiled because we were meant to smile. The passing countryside had the remote look of scenery painted on canvas. I wanted to return to my room and lie still. To my surprise Caroline and I were sent upstairs freely on our own upon our return.

No one followed us. The doors to our rooms lay open. We lingered uncertainly between them.

"Was it too big?" I asked. She knew my mind and that I was speaking of the stable. Transparent shutters came down over her eyes.

"It was naughty," Caroline said. Teeth like pips of a pomegranate showed between her lips. "Why did she?" she asked. There was a childish breathlessness in her voice that I sensed she considered appealing.

I brushed tendrils of golden hair from her forehead. I removed her boater and my own and guided her into my room. A boldness seized me. I closed the door.

"You have to be trained," I said. I knew the words. I felt older. The scent of beyond was in my nostrils. The air was clean in my eyes.

"Why?"

I was truthful. "I do not know, Caroline." We stared at one another. "When Aunt Maude was caning you . . ." I began. I wanted to know.

Caroline said, "It was tight and it stung." The wonder around her mouth was like traces of cream. I kissed her lower lip and sucked it in. A bee's kiss. The tips of our tongues touched and played. My hands held her hips lightly. We both thought of Amanda. I knew that.

"In the linen room. . . ." I said.

Her eyes were hot. "I know . . ." Her form was limp as I began to raise her skirt. My hands sought her stocking tops, the sweet warm flesh above. Caroline placed her hands on my shoulders. "It was nice," she said thickly. A small unravelling of lust was within me. I moved my hands up to the tie of her drawers and loosed it. They sagged, fell to her knees. I knew my wickedness. The curls about her cunny tickled my palm. I felt her moisture.

"You were long in the summerhouse," I said. I had not forgotten. The rolled lips of her slit were oily on my palm. "Was it good?"

Caroline's arms clasped my neck. She seemed about to faint. Her thighs parted so that her knees held her drawers taut. "Yes," she said. I felt dizzy with a sweet sickness. The sea waves lapped us.

"It is good," a voice said. We jerked and clutched one another. I did not want to look. It was Katherine's voice. "But you were told not to—were you not told?" she asked. My hands dropped. Caroline's skirt half fell but remained coiled about her knees. The legs of her fallen knickers showed.

Katherine beckoned me. "I know your devilment," she said and smacked me hard about the bottom. I jumped and squealed as Caroline often squealed. Her hand was as sharp as Father's. There were old photographs in my mind, tinted with dust. The wing of a dead bee on my sleeve.

Caroline sat at command, forlorn. My wrist was gripped. The door to the bedroom left wide open, I was taken upstairs. "The second door," Katherine said. She unlocked it and pushed me roughly within. The room was long and bare. There were cages, the bars of slender ironwork. Three cages in a triangle stood, each the size of a small closet. There were benches, leather-covered. A wooden bar hung across trestles stood in the centre of the floor. Two skylights misted with dust allowed the day to enter.

Katherine stripped me quickly of my dress and drawers and placed me, booted and stockinged, in the nearest cage. I wailed a small wail as the door clanged and closed. A bowl of strawberries and cream, a plate of brown bread and butter and a bottle of white wine lay in the small space at my feet.

Katherine walked to the door. Opening it she glanced back at me and said, "You are lucky, Beatrice. You are the chosen." There was silence and she was gone.

I crouched to eat and drink. There was no spoon with which to eat the strawberries. The cream dripped from my fingers. I licked it. A small drop lay upon the springing of my pussy curls. The wine had been uncorked. I sucked upon the neck of the bottle. The cool gurgling. I did not want the bread.

The door looked at me beyond. It was padded with thick black leather, rimmed all around with metal studs. I liked it. The door would be my friend.

Half an hour passed. I leaned back against the bars and felt one of the cool round rods between the cheeks of my bottom. The sensation was pleasant. I pressed against it but the contact was not as I wished. I could not bend forward.

The door opened. My aunt Maude led Amanda in. Unbound, her dark hair was as long as my own. At her pubis the triangle of curls was crisp and neat. Her stockings were banded at the tops by metal rings. Her long legs teetered in the same mode of high-heeled boots that Caroline and I were made to wear. Her breasts were pale mounds of jellied glory. She held her head high in her nakedness, her pride stung by shame.

"I did not want to come," she blurted. My aunt ignored her. The door of the cage next to mine swung open. On the floor the same meal awaited her that I had received.

"You would not obey—you know you would not obey," my aunt said. The lock clicked. "Beatrice, be still and finish your wine. It is good for you." Her heels sounded loud upon the floor. The studded door closed. All was still. I drank my wine. If there were two bottles I would have poured some over my breasts. I would have raised my nipples to the bars so that Amanda could lick them. Her bottom was quite delicious. Tight and small. Like half a peach it jutted. Had she been tried, trodden, mounted? I was naive then. I should have known that she had not been.

Amanda tried to look at me. She could not. Her hand gripped the bars. Her other arm fell lax. In sagging she showed the sweet curve of her hip.

"It is hateful," she said. She did not ask me who I was. I had wanted her to ask.

"You have not been spanked," I said.

Her eyes were lidded. She had a small, delicate voice. "Have you?" she asked.

"Often." I poured a little wine over my finger and sucked it. I did not want the cage between us. We could have kissed with the cage between us. Her face was oval, cold. There were no mirrors in her eyes. I nibbled a piece of bread. I forgot that I did not want it.

"What will they do?" Amanda asked. Her mouth was small. Under pressure it could be made to kiss with succulence. I like *succulence*. It is like *foutre*.

"They will train you," I said. She stared at me with her mouth open. The metal bands around her thighs fascinated me. They fitted by being slid up her legs where, at the greater swelling, they stopped and gripped as a finger ring does. They had been made for her, she said. She had kicked exceedingly when they were first fitted a month ago. She had been held and had been made to wear them ever since.

"Who fits them?" I asked. She blushed and would not answer. I felt a small inpatience with her. "Drink your wine," I said. She needed to be unlocked, eased, made supple.

The thought stirred me. I was my first revelation.

TWELVE

JENNY appeared and passed my drawers to me through the bars.

"Put them on—your uncle is coming," she said. I scrambled into them just in time. My hands were pious over my breasts.

Uncle did not look at me. Jenny opened Amanda's cage and brought her out. She cowed under his gaze and tried to hide her pubis. Jenny smacked her wrists. There was a strap in my uncle's hand, broad and thick—the same perhaps that our bottoms had tasted in the stable.

Amanda's ankles twisted, causing her to stumble. Jenny took her to the bar which was at waist height. The wood was round and polished. In the centre where her belly would rest was a slight dip.

"Bend and keep your heels together. Grip the lower bar tightly," my uncle told her.

Was his voice more authoritative than the one she had known? Her eyes were dull. For a moment she stared at the wall and then obeyed.

"Please not too hard. May I go then?"

Her voice was a Sunday School voice. Jenny bent and fastened a broad strap round her ankles. Stepping back she glanced at me over her shoulder. I looked at the door, my friendly door. It would grow warm if I leaned against it.

My uncle approached Amanda whose display was quite delicious. Of a purpose, as I realised, her hands were not tied to the lower bar. The orb of her bottom was flawless —the cleft tinted with sepia in its innerness. The strap lifted and uncoiled.

Cra-aaaaack! Ah, the *splat* of it—the deep-kissing leather kiss across her girlish! Amanda winced in anguish, her mouth sagged. A low wail came. The strokes were slow and lazy—insistent. The weight of the leather appeared to need only an indolent movement of arm and wrist. Sometimes it fell across, sometimes under—under the offered apple where the long thighs met and the skin made small creases as if puckering itself in readiness for the outbulge.

Each *splat* brought a higher gasp from her. Her bottom became a haze of pink and white. Her knuckles whitened where they gripped the lower bar.

"Noo-Noo-Noo-Noooooo!" she pleaded. Her hips began to make more violent motions of rejection. At each stroke the tight cheeks tightened. A big man's hands would have encompassed both cheeks together. A split melon. I wanted my tongue to pass around it in its warmth, its heat out-giving, receiving. I counted ten, twelve, fourteen. Amanda gritted her teeth. Was she crying far within herself? The glow of her bottom was luminous, yet no

marks showed. I have since learned the art of it, have heard it called indeed, "French polishing." The leather must never be thin. Thin would be cruel.

The metal bands that held the tops of Amanda's stockings rubbed together. Her knees sagged, making her bottom orb out more. A low whoooo-hoooooing sound hummed from her lips. It is the sound one waits for.

My uncle ceased. I could hear her sobbing, but it was not a sobbing of pain. It was the sobbing of a child who has lost her toys. The sobbing of a child who has ceased to cry when nobody listens.

"Be quiet, Amanda—*Quiet!*"

Jenny's voice was a voice of love. She unfastened the strap around the girl's ankles, drew her legs wide apart and fastened each to the sides of the stand. The salmon-pink of her lovelips showed. Amanda cried out and made to rise, but Jenny took the nape of her neck and forced her down again. My uncle turned away. I wanted him to look at me, to acknowledge my existence, the modesty of my posture with my palms cupped over my breasts. But he did not. He went as one who vaguely recalls an errand to be done. His walk was awkward, stiff. His erection was considerable.

With his exit Aunt Maude appeared. In her hands were a phial of warm, sweet oil and a long thin dildo.

I watched, I listened. I no longer needed to cover my breasts. An oiled finger moved about Amanda's restlessly rolling globe. It sought her rose, her bottom mouth. Jenny's hand was laid now on her down-bent head. All was silence save for her rushing gasps. The dildo when it entered her did so fraction by fraction, upwards between the cheeks, parting their parting.

"Nnnnnnnnn. . . ." Amanda hummed. Her neck and shoulders strained against the pressure of Jenny's hand in vain. Her hips twisted wildly. The dildo rotated slowly in my aunt's fingers, half embedded. Twirling it, she began to glide it back and forth.

"Swcet mare—you will take his piston yet," she murmured. Her voice was without malice. It spoke of hushed rooms, drawn curtains, a muted sun.

"No—oh—OH!"

Amanda's voice rose on a long singsong note, but there was no reply. The dildo entered another inch and then withdrew. Jenny unstrapped her and led her back to the cage. Amanda slumped down sobbing, her face covered. Her elbow tilted the bottle of wine. The neck fell trapped between the bars.

"Why does she cry? We are a benediction," my aunt said.

"They are tears of wrath," Jenny answered. She looked uncertain as if she had collected the wrong words together. She looked to Aunt Maude for refuge. My aunt frowned.

"The spirit of NO is being driven from her," she said. She motioned to my cage. The door was unlocked. I was led without as if I were going to communion. The bar received me. "Caress her first—she is the worthy one," my aunt said.

With my thighs together I was bent as slowly as a mechanism under test. I grasped the bar. My fingers lay upon the ghosts of Amanda's. Jenny's fingers felt for the pouting of my nest, the lovelips pursed. With her free hand she palmed the warm cheeks of my bottom. The upper crease of my slit into which her fingertip wormed, parted just sufficiently to allow her to love-tease my button. I murmured softly in my mind. Pleasure-travellers voyaged through my nerves. The cheeks of my bottom quivered to the urging in-thrust of Jenny's other forefinger.

From the other side of the bar my aunt bent and fondled my breasts very gently as if she were handling hothouse fruit. Her thumbs spoke to my nipples, whispered over them, erected them. Rigid cones on hillocks of snow.

"It is enough—she holds the pose well," Aunt Maude said.

I knew the strap then—knew its bite. Jenny who wielded it permitted me to sway my hips, catching the left cheek as I swayed left—the right as I swayed right. I knew the humming sound in my head—the burgeoning of images, pictures, wickednesses. The heat was tempest to my flesh. I moaned in my undoing.

Twelve? Did I count twelve? My knees sagged. I needed a mouth beneath my open mouth. Amanda was a wax statue in a cage. I parted my knees. The gesture was not unseen.

"Come," Jenny said. There was comprehension in her voice. My moist hand in her cool hand. Wriggling like a schoolgirl I was taken to a divan so narrow that when I lay upon it my legs slipped down on either side.

"Heels firm on the floor—head back," my aunt said. The heavy heat of my bottom weighed upon the black leather beneath.

Jenny moved behind, took my arms and drew them far back above my head. She held me lightly, fearing no rebellion perhaps.

From her sleeve my aunt drew a long white feather with a curving tip. It passed across my vision. My hips jerked.

"No, Beatrice," my aunt intoned. Her words were chiding, soft. The stinging in my bottom from the strap deepened and splurged. "Look at me, Beatrice. Peep your tongue between your lips. Just the tip."

My eyes were Aunt Maude's eyes. They knew countries of the past I had not visited. My tongue peeped. Amanda would lie on her bed at home. The veils of her undoing would be raised. The strap would rise and fall. The metal bands would become gold bands. The roseate hue of her bottom would dwell in his mornings, illuminate his evenings.

"Good . . . so . . . remain . . . do not stir," my aunt admonished me. The feather tickled and moved between my thighs. I bit my lip. My tongue retreated.

My aunt was kind. She waited. A bubble of saliva floated from the re-emerging tip of my tongue. It dwelt on my lower lip. I sang in my throat and felt the twirling of the tip —the white heat of it around my button.

Aunt Maude's eyes dared me to turn from hers. I held. Up, down, the feather teased. It entered me. My buttocks rose, fell, rose again. My eyes were saucers on and on. I writhed—the ceiling in my vision swimming in its blankness. On and on.

I broke the rules.

"Na! Na-Aaaaaah!" I choked.

Starbursts in my belly. My bottom heaved, my heels chattered on the floor. I bucked, absorbing each long inflow of sensations. Starwheels of white heat spun around my clitoris. Out-shooting tendrils of fire swept my body. My tongue protruded. A quivering cry and I slumped, stilled, vacant in frustration. The empty skylights stared at me. A swallow passed across one. Here, now, gone.

In a moment I crouched in my cage again. Amanda and I stared at one another like strangers who have too many questions to ask.

TWELVE

"WERE they good today?" my uncle asked that evening.

We were dressed once more in clinging dresses of the finest wool, our curves displayed. Our boots were thigh-boots. Stockings. Otherwise we were naked beneath.

"They played in the garden. It was sweet to see them playing in the garden," my aunt replied.

Katherine was dressed in black—a high-necked dress. A pearl choker adorned her neck. Jenny was dressed identically. My aunt was less formal in an ordinary day gown. Amanda was absent. We sat formally.

"You may talk," Jenny told us.

Caroline and I looked at one another. We had nothing to say. It was all in the looking. Her nipples peaked through the wool of her dress as did mine. Our globes were outlined. Katherine rose and played softly at the piano. We waited for dinner.

Katherine smiled at us. "They do not talk very much," she said.

My aunt inclined her head. "No—they are lost in their dreams," she replied. She clapped her hands. There was a tinkling, footsteps. It was Amanda. She bore a tray sparkling with glasses. A tiny white lace cap perched on the side of her glossed hair. The pale-pink of her breasts showed through a thin white blouse. The black maid's skirt that she wore had been shortened to show her thighs. With the swaying of its hem the metal rings showed, ringing her black stocking tops.

Walking to my uncle first she bent and offered him a dry sherry. The skirt rose at her bending. Her naked bottom shone pale. No one spoke. When she came to Caroline and me a flush showed on her cheeks. I posted a small smile between her lips. My look was motherly.

Jiggling her bottom cheeks selfconsciously, she left. Our eyes were pasted on the halfmoons of her bottom like mementoes of a journey.

"She will train better here than at home," Aunt Maude said. There was a nodding.

"He will give you jewels," Jenny said and pouted. There was laughter. I contained my own. Caroline's laugh was a small apology of nervousness. My uncle consulted his watch. There was the sound of carriage wheels beyond, a crunching of gravel. The housekeeper flurried to the door. It was Arabella. Her cloak removed in the hallway, she entered in a dull-red dress of silk with elaborate overlays of white lace about the neck. Her diamonds sent messages of light. Without a word she stepped daintily past our chairs like one who is uncertain where to sit. A glass of sherry waited at her elbow.

"The days are good," my aunt said and smiled at her, raising her glass. Caroline and I were as invisible. "You have passed the days well?" It was my uncle's voice.

"There was hunting," Arabella said. She looked faintly bored, as aristocrats often affect to do. Leaning back in her chair she crossed her legs with an audible swishing of silk. "Three girls—pretty and sprightly. They ran not far. We used the walls of the enclosures and the rose garden beyond. They squealed louder than rabbits upon being caught. We pinioned them and carried them within. There were pleasantries. The gentlemen mounted them in turn. They were common girls—field-girls given to such lusts, I believe. Of no account."

Rising, she opened her purse and took out a cigarette from a paper packet. It was not too new a habit then, but few women indulged in it in public. Her hands trembled slightly as she lit it from a candle. The aroma was Turkish.

"You have not behaved. Have you behaved?" Aunt Maude asked her. "The reports have not been good."

The Lady Arabella's face was blurred through smoke. Did Caroline recognise her voice?

"I did not want," Arabella began. Then the gong for dinner sounded. We entered the dining room. Frederick and Amanda served us. Our glasses were refilled constantly. They were the finest wines. My uncle conversed with Aunt Maude and Katherine about the house, the grounds, the farm. There would be a new summerhouse, he said. I squeezed Caroline's thigh. She had the grace to blush. My aunt whispered with Arabella who occasionally shook her head.

"I did not come for this. Will there not be an entertainment?" I heard her ask.

"You know why you were sent again. Disobedience ill becomes you," my aunt told her. Arabella glanced at us for the first time to see if we were listening. Our heads were bowed. We absorbed ourselves in lobster and Chateauneuf du Pape.

"They were blindfolded before," Arabella muttered.

My aunt waved her hand. "It is of no account," she said, "come, you must permit at least a little display." Rising, she moved behind Arabella, bent over her and unbuttoned her dress at the front. I saw the purpose of its buttoning there. As the sides slid away her breasts were lifted out in all their splendour. Her nipples were rouged. Katherine slid her chair back and did the same to Caroline and I. Aunt Maude smiled, took her seat once more and brought a goblet of wine to Arabella's lips. Her throat worked as she drank.

"So you must sit in future when you return—it is more seemly," my aunt told her.

Amanda entered. Frederick followed and cleared away our plates. He went out. In Amanda's hand was a silver jug.

"You have brought the cream?" Katherine asked her. "It is warm?"

Amanda nodded. There was bemusement in her face. A cloud of unknowing lay upon her features. Her lips were rouged, her eyes shadowed. She looked beautiful, I thought. At the flaring of her skirt as she passed I saw faint pink marks upon her bottom cheeks. The hem fell like a broken promise and then lifted again. She approached Katherine's side.

"Not here—to the Lady Arabella," Katherine said impatiently. My aunt's hands disappeared beneath the table at Arabella's side. Arabella's face suffused. Her body seemed to lift a little. There was a loud rustling of silk. Her skirt had been drawn up. Amanda's footsteps were quick, small and elegant as she moved around the long table to Arabella.

She appeared to be learning quickly—in hope, no doubt, that she would be released. Would she run to the woods and hide? There would be a hunting. She would be trussed and taken home, her skirt wound upwards amid the tight cords.

"Pour," my aunt said. She appeared to grip Arabella's hand nearest to her own beneath the tablecloth.

Arabella gave a start, her chair creaked. Amanda had bent and poured the warm, rich cream between the valley of her breasts, the deep divide. I wanted to rise and see its trickling—the white lava. I dared not.

"Be still—it will flow down—let it flow," my aunt told Arabella.

A balloon of smoke from my uncle's cigar floated over the table. We were virginal in our sitting, Caroline and I. We looked and did not look.

"Down, girl!" my aunt said to Amanda. Their eyes clashed like rapiers. The jug was empty. Its creaming oozed its last over the lip. Falteringly Amanda placed it on the table. Her knees bent. She disappeared. Beneath the polished table of oak I felt her. Her bottom nudged my toe. Arabella's eyes rolled, she leaned back. A soft gasp. I could feel her legs open, guided no doubt by my aunt's busy hands. The warm cream made a white trail down between her luscious breasts and disappeared beneath the looseness of her dress where Aunt Maude had slipped the tie at her waist.

"You liked the horses?" It was my uncle's voice. He addressed me.

"Yes, Uncle." Caroline said yes uncle in turn. The wine bottles passed. Our glasses were refilled.

"Let us be quiet for a moment," my aunt admonished as if we had been chattering constantly.

I wanted my boot to slide off—to feel with my stockinged toes the bulge of Amanda's bottom as she knelt, her face most obviously now between Arabella's thighs. Tasting cream. Cream on her bush, her pouting, her sticky.

Arabella gave a little jump. Her eyes half closed. "Drink your wine," my aunt told her. The goblet was raised to her lips anew. Her lips slurped. Beneath my feet there came another slurping. Arabella bubbled and spluttered into her goblet.

"Mounted but twice indeed since you visited," my aunt said to her scoldingly. "Are you not bad, my love?"

Arabella's eyes closed. She moved her lips away pettishly from the goblet. Wine spilled its fall on to her breasts. "P. . . p. . . p. . . p. . . ." Little explosions of sound from her mouth. Her hips worked, breasts jiggling. The slurping noise beneath the table increased.

"Such ripeness—it is always pretty to see," Katherine murmured. She emptied the rest of her wine into my uncle's glass. He drank upon it immediately. My aunt glared at her. Katherine smiled. For a moment I thought she would embrace me but instead she got up and passed around behind me to Caroline. Bending over her and drawing her face round, she covered Caroline's mouth with her own and passed her fingertips suavely about the snowy hillocks which stood revealed. I could feel the tingling in my mouth of my sister's nipples. Katherine's tongue delved. I could feel it delve.

The feet of Arabella's chair were scraping. The chair rocked.

"You are difficult, too, Caroline, are you not?" Katherine purred. Her mouth was a rose. Would I ever kiss her fully? She desired to make me jealous, I know. The sound of Amanda's lapping tongue was in my ears. Small noises of hysterical sound wisped from Arabella's lips. My aunt held her.

"Look at me, Caroline—haven't you been difficult?" Katherine coaxed.

"Ye . . . ye . . . yesssssss," Caroline gritted. "Oh, but it was so big and. . . ."

"What nonsense she speaks," my aunt laughed, "you have sucked it—I know you have. Amanda, rise, leave her!"

A scuffling, Amanda appeared, face hot, lips wet. My uncle beckoned her. Her skirt, caught up, betrayed the wantonness of her bare bottom.

"Your report was no better. Worse, indeed," he told her. "Is it not true?"

"Sir?" Amanda asked thickly. Her eyes were bleared, her expression slightly vacant. I expected him to draw her forward and fondle her bottom. To my surprise he did not. I thought of Father. He lay on the beach, perhaps, his cutlass limp, fallen. Pebbles stirred as people approached and stared down at him. He rested in his waiting.

A murmuring beside me, a soft moist sound of lips. I hated Caroline. She was shy. She had sucked the liqueur of love—the sperm had inundated her mouth. She had lain on her bed naked, her thighs apart. Her nest had waited for his eggs to nestle against it. I would whip her.

Arabella lay back against the high back of her chair. Her mouth was open, a look of languishing upon her face. I judged her about twenty-seven. Her hand wore no wedding ring. Her fingernails glistened, perfectly manicured. My aunt's hand worked gently beneath the table, between her thighs. Arabella's eyelashes fluttered.

My uncle waved his cigar. "Take her upstairs," he said to Katherine. Led out in docile tread, Caroline did not look back. Footsteps on the stairs. Katherine returned.

"As to Amanda. . . ." Katherine said. Everyone waited for her to speak except perhaps Arabella who was floating still in a luxury of sensations. "Amanda, stand in the corner there facing us. How wicked you have been!"

My aunt rang a bell. Frederick entered. He carried a small silver bucket wherein stood a wine bottle packed around with ice. Placing it on the table, he removed the bottle, wiped it with a napkin and left it there. The door closed again behind him. The cork of the bottle was round, black and polished.

"Lift your skirts—part your legs," Katherine ordered. My uncle did not turn to look. Amanda's eyes were lanterns. The black flaring of her bush. The curls looked thicker now. The creamy tint of her flat belly.

"Wicked!" Katherine intoned. She took the bottle and moved to Amanda whose eyes hunted the ceiling. The neck of the bottle lowered and hovered beneath her pubic mound. It hung in a straight line down between her stockinged thighs. "Draw your legs together, Amanda—grip it!"

A long hush-rushing sound like a sudden movement of water surged from Amanda's throat. Her eyes screwed up. Her long eyelashes trembled. Ice-cold, the bottle was gripped between her trembling thighs. Expressionless, Katherine placed her fingers delicately beneath the base of the bottle and urged it gently up.

"*Noooo-Aaaaah!*" Amanda moaned. The black, round shiny cork parted her lovelips and was gripped within it.

Katherine drew down the tiny skirt.

"*Whooooo!*" Amanda jittered. Her skirt hid all but the base of the bottle. Her teeth chattered. Small pearls of white. I want to run my teeth around them.

"Finish the wine," my uncle said. He rose—an avuncular host—and filled our glasses. Arabella's head had sunk. Her spirit moved through forests afar. The cream had long been lapped from her slit, her tight-purse, her nutcracker, her penis-pouter. Her bottom cheeks relaxed in their fullness, naked upon her seat.

I dipped the tip of my tongue in my glass. It swam like a goldfish. I wanted to French-drink again. Was it forbidden? Arabella had opened her eyes and sat up. She seemed more composed. Her head inclined towards Aunt Maude's. Sitting beside me again, Katherine slid her hand on to my thigh and caressed it. I would not look at her. I cast my eyes down upon the tablecloth, the white, the serene.

"Are we loved?" she asked me. My mind had already begun to catch at the corners of reason. Amanda stood in her aloneness. I did not reply. I wanted to catch the words my aunt was speaking. Of them all, the Lady Arabella intrigued me most. Her coming was totally voluntary, I felt. Her body held an arrogance of desire, unfulfilled until it was drawn forth by persuasion. Were we all the same? To what dark altars were we led? Darkness was strawberries —the sunlight cream.

"It excites me—I fear it," Arabella said.

"The root of desire is fearing. When you were caught with your drawers down, did you not intend to be caught?"

"I was dragged to my room," Arabella muttered. Her voice contained a sulkiness of satisfaction.

"And mounted admirably," my aunt said dryly, "as you were here, after your birching. You prefer to be birched?"

"Not always, but the strap. . . ."

"It subdues you, yes, but you must not grow reliant upon it. Marriage will be no cure for you. It will dilute the very qualities that give you such attraction, my dear. I shall recommend that you are blindfolded in future. It will enclose such modesty as you have."

My aunt twirled the stem of her wine glass. Even as I, she stared at the tablecloth and appeared to muse. "As I recall," she continued, "there is a particular manservant in your house. Is he not called Eric? He is young, lusty. During the act, when your bottom is bared, he will present his to your mouth. Blindfolded you will grope for it even while you are being pistoned. . . ."

A cry from Arabella interrupted my aunt. She covered her face. "Oh! I could not!" she burst.

Aunt Maude rose. "Thomas, you will entertain her," she announced. "Amanda, you may go to the kitchen, girl." Her glance encompassed Katherine, Jenny and myself. The drawing room received us. We stood. Parts of the furniture had been cleared away, leaving a space in the centre of the floor. There stood a chair—a black leather one that I had never seen before. It was a simple affair. The strong wooden legs were strutted and rose some three feet. The broad seat —if it could be called one—was a mere sling of leather. Where the uprights of the back rose, another strong width of leather was repeated. In the centre of it was a small hole. Facing the chair so that the fronts of the seats touched was an identical one. In general aspect it was like a crude couch without a back to it. I had seen such in ancient Egyptian relics.

We stood. Beside me, Jenny caressed the bulbous curve of my bottom cheeks lightly. Katherine went into the hall and returned shortly. Frederick came with her. He was naked. His prong pronged. Around his neck was a halter to which a chain was attached.

Unspeaking, Katherine led him to the rear of one of the chairs and turned him to face it. His eyes were blind in their unseeing. His balls swung. "Closer!" Katherine snapped at him. His feet shuffled forward, the chain clinking. With a slight grimace of his features, the knob of his erect penis touched the leather sling-back. To a slight but disdainful guidance of Katherine's fingers the knob passed through the hole and continued its upward glide until his prick emerged completely on the other side, facing the back of the other chair.

Motionless he stood, the veins raised on his tool which seemed to swell more by the tight enclosure. His balls pressed against the leather below the aperture.

Jenny's fingers quested beneath my bottom, pressing the thin wool up between my cheeks. I strained my legs and endeavoured to stand still. Aunt Maude entered, surveyed the scene and nodded. A faint scuffling of heels came and Arabella was patted and persuaded within by my uncle. Her grown was wreathed up to her hips, her eyes blindfolded. Her legs were superb: statuesque, long, and beautifully curved. The fluff of her cunny was thick with curls. Her thighs rubbed nervously as she stumbled forward.

"It is a simulation," Jenny murmured to me.

Guided by my aunt's hands, Arabella was taken to the chairs and made to kneel upon the seats. But an inch before her mouth—had she but known it then—the servant's prick jutted its menace. Her magnificent bottom cheeks—cheeks such as Michelangelo might have carved in marble—pressed against the back of the other chair. The waiting hole there appeared to centre itself exactly in line with the deep divide between her hemispheres. Melon-full, her exposed breasts hung down. Her knees made to shift in nervous reflex, but the dipping of the sling-seat into which the weight of her legs pressed permitted little movement.

My uncle approached the back of the chair to which her haunches were pressed. His face had a haggard aspect. His jacket and waistcoat had been removed. The top of his breeches was unbuttoned.

"Not yet—you are not privileged," Jenny said. With a last searching caress her hand relinquished my bottom. In my emptiness I stood while she blindfolded me, voices around me. How strange in the darkness of my dark. Did the furniture move—the sideboard menace? I had imaginings. A mystic magic.

"Hold her hips." It was my uncle's groan.

"There is no need, Thomas. She will be birched if she moves, save in desiring. Open your mouth now, Arabella —feel for it, absorb the knob—now press your bottom back, tight to the leather. Thomas, now!"

Groans, gurgles, cries—a gurgling, a moan. A blubbering, a slap, a sucking sound. Her mouth corked. Her lips would puff around the servant's tool. Creak of wooden legs. A croaking whine from Arabella. Her bottom corked in turn.

In my impossibilities I swayed. But feet away from me the thin inhissing of breath sounded through Arabella's nostrils. Tomorrow perhaps she would receive guests for tea. The polite questions of everydayness would be asked. Music sheets would lay decoratively ranged upon a piano. Her parents would flank her sides. It would be known that she was obedient. The servants would move quietly in their domain. The curtains would be dumb to speak. Her bed would wait for night to fall. Sperm-drops around her stocking tops. Was here salvation? Her eyes would be hollow, receiving messages.

"Ah! in her to the root. She has taken both." It was Katherine's voice. Her tongue licked in my ear. I trembled. I knew I must stand still. In my stillness standing.

No one would ever know. Beyond our circles, no one. We were the chosen, the receptors of lust in our desiring.

THIRTEEN

THE laurel leaves of the garden hedge were dry. I moved my cheek against them. The breeze fluttered my skirt. For two hours on the following morning we had been caged, Caroline, Amanda and I. Then Jenny had taken us out one by one and accorded us twelve strokes of the strap across our naked bottoms.

"Your morning exercise—you may be given more pleasant ones shortly," she said. Amanda blubbered quietly. Each of us sank down in our cage again, our bottoms seared. We were not to talk, we were told.

Released first and dressed, this time in a white wool dress with a gold chain at my waist, I was sent into the garden. I loitered palely. My hands toyed with twigs. The maidservant Mary brought out lemonade. It cooled my body with a sheet of cold within. My eyes were quiet against her own. I felt intimations of newness within me.

Father on the high seas sailing. I would write to him. By fast packet-ship my letter would arrive shortly after his landing. I returned within the house, not knowing whether I was permitted to return, and asked my aunt. The space where the two leather seat-supports had been the night before was now filled again by a small table. Bric-a-brac and vases stood upon it. I looked for the impress of the feet of the chairs in the carpet but saw none.

Aunt Maude sat embroidering. I asked if I might write. Her expression issued surprise. I would find paper, pen and ink already placed in my room, she said. As I made to go she beckoned me. I stood close. Her hand passed up beneath the clinging of my dress—perhaps to satisfy her that I was wearing no drawers.

"How firm and fleshy you are," she said, and sighed. The heat of the strap was still in my bottom. It communicated itself to her fingertips. Her hand slipped down, caressing the backs of my thighs as it went. "Write well and clearly," she told me.

I ascended to my room. All was put ready for me as if it had been anticipated. A small escritoire stood against one wall. I seated myself and drew the paper toward me. The ink was black. I swirled it gently with the decorated steel nib of the pen. "Dearest Father. . . ." A bird's wings rustled against the window. I rose, but it was gone. No message lay upon the sill. I leaned my forehead against the glass. "Dearest Father. . . ."

I started and turned at the sudden entrance of Katherine.

"There is nothing to say," she said, "it is all in the doing."

"It is not true," I said. I wanted to cry. Her arms enfolded me lightly as one embraces a child who must leave soon upon a feared journey.

"It is good that you know. If you had not known you would be writing swiftly. Is that not so?"

Her voice coaxed. I nodded against her shoulder. A simple movement of her supple form sufficed to bring her curves tightly against mine. Half swooning I moved my belly in a sinuous sleeking against her own. She released me too quickly with a smile that I could feel passing over my own mouth in its passing.

"There is to be a reception. Brush your hair, wear a boater—it suits you," Katherine said. She waited while I obeyed. Descending, she took hat and gloves from Mary who stood waiting. Two horses pawed the dust outside. This time the carriage was a hansom.

"May Caroline not come?" I asked. My question was ignored. I entered first, followed by Katherine who sat close beside me.

"We are going to see a friend," she said.

The journey took an hour. We passed the house where Amanda lived. The children with the hoops had gone. They sat in some small schoolhouse, perhaps, learning the directions of rivers and the trade winds. Katherine had not conversed with me except to ask if I was thirsty. When I nodded we reined in at an inn. A potboy brought us out mugs of ale. The coachman quaffed his own loudly. With a belching from above and a cracking of the whip we were off again.

The house at which we arrived lay like my uncle's in rural isolation. Stone columns adorned with Cupids ranged at the entrance. The drive was long and straight. Immediately the hansom braked, a butler appeared and ushered us in with the grave mien of one who has important people to announce. We entered a drawing room where, to my astonishment, Arabella sat picking at crochet work. From a chair facing her own, the man with the military moustache who I had seen with her before rose and greeted us. Arabella nodded politely and smiled at Katherine. Her long fingers worked elegantly.

The gentleman, whose name was Rupert, drew Katherine aside to the end of the long room. I caught but a few words of their whisperings. "It will progress her," I heard him say. I glanced at Arabella. Her lips had pursed tightly. I perceived a slight tremor of her fingers.

Katherine turned back to me. "We shall go upstairs," she said. I wondered in my wonderings. The room was one of great charm. An Adams fireplace stood resplendent. Two small lions carved in stone rested on either side of the big brass fender. Blue velvet drapes were abundant. The furniture smelled of newness.

Katherine's voice seemed to encompass Arabella also. Her hands flirted with the piece of crochet work and fell. The gentleman spoke her name. She got up, her eyes uncertain. The lacework fluttered to the floor. Preceding us he advanced into the hallway and up the wide, curving staircase. There, at the first landing, several doors faced us as did also three young girls in servant attire who appeared to be in-waiting. They stood side by side against a wall. Their hands were bound behind them, their mouths gagged. Their black dresses, white aprons and morning caps were of the utmost neatness.

"This one," Katherine said. She selected the smallest girl who looked about seventeen, her fulsomeness evident in the sheathing of her dress about her curves.

Rupert jerked his head and the girl detached herself and followed us, her gait made slightly awkward by her bound wrists.

We ascended again to the second floor where a lady of

singular beauty, in her middle years, appeared as if to descend. She halted and appraised us. "A progression, yes," she echoed as the gentleman spoke to her, "it will be good for her. Arabella, you will obey, my dear." Kissing her on the cheek she passed on and down. To untie the other two maids, I thought. I knew their posture, the inward-seeking of their thoughts, the tightness of their bottom cheeks. Their thighs would tremble in the mystery of their beings.

A door opened. We entered a room that was longer than the drawing room beneath. Four windows ranged along the farther wall, the drapes drawn back. The double doors closed heavily. Arabella, the maid and I were ushered to the centre of the room.

I saw then the paintings which hung along the wall facing the windows. There were men and girls in bonds. The men exhibited penises that were either bound in leather or protruded boldly in their nakedness. Each vein was so cunningly painted that one could have touched and felt the slight swellings. Women lay bound, naked or in curious attire, one upon the other. Men with their wrists bound and their eyes blindfolded knelt in their penis-seeking between the splayed thighs of naked ladies.

My eyes passed through them as if through mirrors. Except for one. It was of a girl who wore thigh boots and black tights. The tights had been lowered to her knees. Each hair of her pubic curls had been painted separately with the finest of brushes. She was bound to a post that stood alone in the centre of a planked floor. She wore no gag. Her head was upright and her eyes proud. Her long golden hair was as mine. The cherry nipples of her breasts peaked their proudness.

Katherine moved beside me. "It is better to be bound than to see others bound, is it not?" she asked me. I sought

Arabella's eyes but she would not look. Her white dress was as simple as my own. I divined her nudity beneath.

"I do not know," I murmured.

"Come—we shall know the answer," Katherine replied. Close to the far end of the room a stout post stood, even as in the painting. To the back of it was fastened four lengths of wood in the shape of a square that protruded on either side. Led forward, I was turned so that my back came against the post.

"Raise your arms," Katherine instructed. I did so. My wrists came against the lengths of wood. Taking cords she bound them so that I was held as on a cross. "He will not have seen you before," Katherine said and threw a smile over her shoulder at Rupert who had moved closely behind Arabella. I watched her head jerk nervously as he palmed her bottom.

Katherine bent and raised my dress, coiling the wool up until it wreathed tightly about my hips. My pubis bared, I blinked and endeavoured to stare past the pair facing me, but the increasing wriggling of Arabella's hips was lure to my eyes.

Drawn wide apart, my ankles were next secured. The lips of my slit parted stickily, warmed and moistened as they had been by our journey. Arabella murmured and choked a small cry. Her dress was being slowly lifted at the back by Rupert. The maid stood like a small tree waiting.

Katherine beckoned her. In her awkwardness she came. Katherine pushed her to her knees before me and removed her gag.

"Have you taught her to lick?" she asked Rupert, whose hands were now busy beneath the back of Arabella's dress. The young woman blushed deeply but seemed frozen to the spot. At the back her bottom was now bared, lush and full in all its proud paleness. At the front the material of her dress looped with some modesty still to hide her pussy.

Rupert shook his head. With such treasures of firm flesh as bulged into his hands, he was equally entranced by the vision I presented.

"Dearest Father. . . ."

The paper lay forlorn where I had left it. No signals flew. At the first touch of the maid's nose to my belly I quivered in my longings. Katherine nudged her and she sank lower as one who makes to drink from a tap.

She kissed my knees. Her mouth absorbed itself above and circled in an O about my thighs. Her lips teased the tight banding of my stocking tops. Her tongue sought the soft-firm flesh of my inner thighs. I bent my knees slightly. I offered, sought. As through crazed glass I watched Rupert's hands desert Arabella's bottom and glide beneath her armpits to unfasten the front of her dress.

I wanted her. Her mouth, her tongue. I sought to reach her with my eyes, but hers were dazed. As her breasts were bared she whimpered and struggled. Pink of face he held her. Her nipples extended through his fingers. The jellied mounds stirred beneath his seekings.

I felt the outflicking of the maid's tongue ere it reached me, touched my lovelips. I wanted not to moan. I must not moan. Thumbs parted my lips and sought my clitoris, my button, my ariser. The tongue tip swirled. I knew its cunning. Ah! she was good. Starshells burst in my belly. I whimpered, ground my hips. Her tongue would not reach into me. I wanted it.

Did I cry out? On the brink of my salty spray, my spilling, I tremored in a cloud of delight.

"There is nothing to say. It is all in the doing," Katherine had said. Arabella was as one swooning. The arms of Rupert upheld her. Her dress was raised in front—her thighs, her longing. Her bush was plump—a perfect mound of Venus. Had it been creamed, or only her bottom yet? I knew the answer soon.

"Enough!" Katherine said. She stirred the maid with her foot. The girl fell back and twisted sideways. Her shoulder bumped the floor. Her small pink tongue licked around her lips.

Arabella's struggles renewed at Katherine's turning. Her eyes were wild as hunted fawns. Traitorous, her nipples shone erect. Her thighs clenched together. Her stockings of light grey silk rubbed. The noise made an electric hissing. Did she not know it as an invitation?

I held upon my cross. The maid beneath me did not stir save to glance slyly up between my legs. I used the coldness of my eyes upon her. She blushed and hid her eyes. They were eyes that would move and rustle in the grass at night. In her truckle bed she would lie at evening beneath a coarse blanket. Upon heavy footsteps waiting. A cottage smallness. The cramped places of lust. A heaving of loins. Jettings of desire. Globules of sperm upon her pussy hairs. Small legs, perfectly shaped, stirred beneath her skirt.

I would buy her, perhaps.

"NO!"

Arabella screamed foolishly as she was borne to a couch of purple velvet, her dress raised high to bare her belly.

"*Wha-aaaaah!*" Her screams became hysteria as Katherine assisted in thrusting her down, mounting upon her shoulders as she had mounted upon my face. Wildly as Arabella kicked she could not escape the scooping back of her knees by Katherine. Her slit showed pulpy in its fullness.

For the battle now Rupert prepared, casting off his jacket and lowering his breeches. His cockprong pronged a full nine inches long. The head was purplish, swollen. His hands assisted Katherine's in parting Arabella's long milky thighs. Arabella's shoulders bucked. She was held. Her anguished cries half-extinguished beneath Katherine's skirt bubbled away.

"You have had her bottom only?" Katherine asked.

"Thrice—including her penance over the table when she was birched. How magnificent she looks!"

For long moments while Arabella blindly squirmed her hips, he gazed upon the fount of his desiring. I wanted the maid again—her tongue. In my proudness I did not ask. Only the silent pulsing of my quim beseeched.

With a groan he was entered.

"Slowly—slowly," Katherine breathed. An eagle perched, she gazed upon the conquest—the curl-fringed lips that rolled in succulence, parting to the charger's crest. Arabella's thighs quivered in their grip. Hands scooped her bottom, the strength of him lifting her.

Inklings of surrender I sensed even as the veined shaft sank within. Inklings. It is a pretty word. Small notes of sound spattered with ink. The acquiescence of her bottom stirred me. It shifted little on his cupping palms once she was shafted to the full.

My instincts were shared, it seemed. Of a sudden, Katherine dismounted from the nubile beauty who held the cock full-clenched within her now. Puffed of cheeks that were sheened with moisture, Arabella stirred but faintly. His belly pressed upon hers. Their pubic hairs mingled. I could feel his throbbing as within myself—the gently ticking impulse of desire.

Arabella succumbed. Elegant in their fullness, her stockinged legs slid down from his loosing grasp. The heels of her boots stirred upon the velvet of the couch. Her legs trembled and straightened. Her large breasts, tumbled out of her opened dress, gave her a perfect aspect of voluptuousness.

His breeches slid farther down. He whispered, as I thought, something in her ear. Her face was deeply flushed. Her lips moved. Her hands clasped timourously at his shirt.

"Your tongue," he husked, "your tongue now, Arabella."

Her breath scooped in audibly as if drawn by some inward suction in her throat.

"You must not come! Oh! You must not come!"

The couch jolted, stirred. The pleasure train of pleasure had begun.

Her tongue protruded, thrust within his mouth. Their mouths gobbled. Glistening, his shaft emerged—sank in again. Rocking, creaking. His pace quickened. Her knees bent as if shyly at first. Her calves lifted, uncertain in their seeking. In a moment, his cock pounding her with virile force, they were knotted about his loins. A squelching. Their tongues worked. Moaning they squirmed their loins.

The maid who lay at my feet stirred. She had not the vision of them in her eyes. Awkwardly she struggled to her knees.

Katherine, whose absorption in the lustful scene was as my own, even so swung her head around.

"No!" she snapped. "Stand by the door—your back to us."

The girl obeyed. Out of the corners of her eyes as she passed the couch she watched the threshings of desire. He was long at his task—longer than I had deemed he could hold in his excitement. Then at last his rattling cry—a swift tightening of Arabella's legs. Her breasts were at pillage. He sucked upon them greedily in his coming, his outspurting. Judders, quivers, a last tight clenching of her cuntlips. Then was stillness.

Arabella's head lay back, her eyes and mouth open. Her

legs slackened, fell. Her entire body seemed to quiver at the withdrawal of his cock which left a snail's trail of sperm down her thigh. Her face held a look of vacant surprise. Made to rise at last, her dress caught up, she leaned against him foolishly.

"Tonight again," he said. He patted her bottom. Her eyes would not look at my eyes. Turning away she patted haplessly at her hair and then covered herself. I knew her wetness.

"In your silences shall you be saved, Beatrice," Katherine murmured to me. There was approval in her look. Releasing me, she fussed about my tidiness like a nurse.

The maid, ignored, was left to her own devices. Sedately we descended, walking quietly as people entering a theatre after the curtain has risen. In the drawing room the lady we had encountered above sat drinking wine. A maid entered and filled the glasses that awaited us on a sideboard.

"Arabella—you dropped your crochet on the floor," the lady said. Her tone was reproachful. Rupert had not followed us into the room, I noticed. His orgasm must have been excessive on their first such bout.

"I am sorry," Arabella replied in a muted voice. She picked it up from where it lay and took it upon her lap again. There was a flush on her cheeks but otherwise she appeared composed again.

We sat drinking our wine and spoke of mundane things.

FOURTEEN

"AH, how she was fucked!" Katherine said as we entered the hansom again.

I had never heard such coarseness. I stared at her. Her eyes had a light in them I had not seen before.

"Should not he have fucked her—spilled his semen within her richness? When he buggered her, over the table —ah, how we had to hold her—his cock disappearing within her cleft. Come, kiss me, Beatrice!"

Her arm enfolded my shoulders. Our lips met in a haze of sweetness. Deep her long tongue delved within my mouth. The jolting of the carriage added to the excitement of our embrace. I felt her hand pass up beneath my skirt. I parted my thighs to her seeking. Her thumb brushed the lips of my slit. I choked my little gasps within her mouth.

"Seven years—seven years it has taken him to bring her to that—yet she obeys us now. He will fuck her again tonight. How timid she will be at first, how flushed! His tongue will lick at her nipples, stir her being. Her thighs will move awkwardly, seeking to be opened and yet not. Their tongues will meet. Falteringly her hand will find his cock. She adores bottom fucking now, though he has had her that way but thrice, each time held down. She will come to the strap and birch more easily now, knowing her reward —the slug of flesh within her bottom gripped. Do you hear me, Beatrice?"

I could not hear. I knew not her wording. My slit creamed, bubbled, spurting. Sliding from the carriage seat, I all but fell on the floor. My dignity, my being, lay scattered about me like dying petals. I clasped her, in my falling clasped.

"I love you," I said.

Katherine laughed and pushed me roughly into the corner. Her fingers glistened. Would she lick them?

"Did you not like my litany?" she asked.

I nodded. The words had been thrown at me out of a box. I had caught them yet I needs must arrange them. A sullenness crossed my features. I wanted to cry. I sought greater fulfilment. Cock. He had lain upon her and given her his cock. I hated the crudities. I shuttered them off in my mind. They tapped at the shutters. I ignored them.

Katherine's eyes were mocking. "You did not like it?" she asked.

Was I under test? I shook my head. "I do not know," I said.

Katherine laughed. "You fool. There are clues. You have not found them yet, Beatrice. Be silent now. Await the teaching."

Dinner that evening was formal. Caroline sat quiet,

attentive. She had been a good girl, my aunt said. Amanda, it seemed, was caged upstairs, her meal taken to her. I wore black, the wool clinging as tightly as ever. There was a new serving maid, a woman of about thirty, comely and plump. The dull black dress and white apron suited her. During the whole meal she was not required to say a word. I wondered if she had eaten and drunk before us. Such things engage my mind sometimes. It is a kindness. Father told me once that it was my old-fashioned way.

We took coffee in the lounge, then turned to liqueurs. There was a festive air. I could feel it. We lounged at our ease. The shackles were cast. Caroline laughed occasionally with Uncle. We were tamed.

When the maid brought in the Cointreau, Katherine took her wrist.

"Drink with us," she said.

"M'am?" The maid's cheeks coloured.

"Drink with us—sit with us—here at my feet—take a glass." Katherine's words were pellets. They stung against my skin. The woman skimmed a nervous look around where we sat in a circle.

"Look, I will hold your glass while you sit," Aunt Maude told her.

The maid obeyed at last, discomforted in her sitting on the floor. Her legs coiled under her. I liked the shape of her calves. Her ankles were slender. Slender ankles and plump thighs often betoken sensuousness to some degree.

"Lean back and be comfortable," Aunt Maude said. She dropped a cushion onto the carpet for the maid to lean upon. She looked like a houri—an odalisque. Uncle was whispering to Caroline. What were they saying?

"Attractive women often sit on the floor," Katherine remarked. The maid looked at her and did not know whether to smile or not. Katherine's smile was a cat's smile. With a flip of her toes she kicked off one of the gold Turkish slippers she was wearing and, to the woman's startlement, laid her toes on her thigh. Her toes curled.

"It is nice," Katherine said. Her foot moved upwards along the maid's hip and felt its curving. "Drink your drink," she said sharply. The woman obeyed. My aunt eased a shoe off in turn. Sitting obliquely behind the maid she lifted her leg, eased her stockinged foot beneath the woman's chin and lifted it.

"Lie down—down!" my aunt said.

The maid's arm made a querulous seeking gesture, but she obeyed. The cushion squeezed itself from under her. Katherine circled her leg and moved the sole of her foot lightly over the woman's prominent breasts. She started and would have sat up if Aunt Maude's foot had not then moved with a twist of ankle to the front of her neck.

The maid's eyes bulged.

"M'am—I don't want to," she whined.

"Oh, be quiet!" Katherine said impatiently. Her foot slid back down. Her toes hooked in the hem of the maid's skirt and drew it up above her stocking tops. Plump thighs gleamed. The simple garters she wore bit tightly into her flesh.

"No, please, M'am."

Neither listened. Aunt Maude's toes were caressing her neck and up behind her ear. Katherine's toes delved upwards beneath the hang of the upflipped skirt. The woman's hands scrabbled on the carpet. My aunt's toes soothed over her mouth. A choking little cry and the maid's back arched. The delicate searching movements of Katherine's toes up between her thighs made the black material ripple. The maid's cheeks were pink. Her lips parted beneath the sole of my aunt's foot which rubbed suavely, skimming her mouth. Katherine's toes projected up into the skirt. Her heel was rubbing now.

The maid moaned and closed her eyes. Beside me, Caroline puffed out her breath. The maid's eyes closed. Her bottom worked slightly. She drew up one knee. My uncle's eyes were strangely incurious. Aunt Maude slipped down on to her knees beside the maid and began unbuttoning the front of her dress. The ripe gourds of her breasts came into view. Her nipples were stark and thick in their conical rising.

Katherine slid down onto her knees in turn. Her hands swept the skirt of the maid's dress up to her waist. A bulge of pubic hairs sprouted thickly. The maid covered her face and made little cries.

"Open your legs properly!" Katherine told her sharply. Still with her eyes covered the maid began to edge her ankles apart. It would be her first such pleasuring, perhaps, though female servants who shared bedrooms frequently fingered one another.

Uncle loomed up before me. He smiled, drew my hand towards him.

"We shall go upstairs," he said. I was bereft. Caroline would see. I would not see. We entered the hall and ascended. I did not want to go in the cage. But the room was empty and the cages were empty. "Go to the bar—raise your dress," my uncle said.

I wanted to see what would happen to the maid. Would she be ripe in her desiring? I did not want Katherine to kiss her. But I obeyed. A bulbous symphony in black and white. I gripped the lower bar, my bottom bared to him. He knew me in his seeing now. The door reopened but I did not look. Footsteps quiet. Tapering fingers, coated with warm oil, massaged the groove of my pumpkin. At my rose, my O, the finger lingered, soothing. High heels clicked again and our visitor was gone.

Strained in my posture I kept my thighs, my heels together. The purse of my love-longing peeped its figlike shape beneath my cheeks. I waited.

At the first crack of the leather I cried out my small cry, my head hung. The stinging of the strap assailed me three, four, five, six times. I clenched my nether cheeks, their plumpness hot. Tears oozed.

The quiver-cry that burst next from me was at the first biting of three dozen thongs. My whip had come—it lived —it sang. I hated, loved it.

"Uncle, don't!"

My little wail, the dying cry. I choked in my choking sobs. The tips of the thongs sought me, burnished the blossoming of my cheeks and sought the crevices. Rain of fire, down-showering of sparks. My hips squirmed, my heels squeaked on the floor. Master of my arching beauty now, he stung me deeper till my sobs came louder. My shoulders lifted, fell. My hands slipped on the bar and gripped anew.

At the dropping of the whip at last—betraying clatter on the floor—I made to rise. My hand reached back and sought my upcast dress.

"No, Beatrice, stay!"

"No more!"

My bottom scorched, my wail beseeched. Hands at my hips. They gripped like steel.

"Down, Beatrice, down!"

The cheeks of my bottóm held, parted, spread. My rose exposed. "*No-ooooh!*" The last cry of my frailty fluttered, fell. I felt the flare of body heat, his cock. The knob-cock of him, oozing in. Breath whistling from my throat, I made to rise.

"Down, Beatrice—down, girl, *down*!"

I blubbered, squirmed. I wanted, did not want. The rubbery ring of my anus yielded to invasion—the swollen plum, indriving of his prick. Quarter inch by quarter inch the veined shaft entered. My mouth gaped. The thick peg throbbed, its urging urged within. Then with a groan he sheathed it to the full, my brazen cheeks a butterball of heat to his belly.

Within me now it stirred, pulsed, throbbed. His balls nestled under my slit. Then he withdrew—the slow unsheathing I both feared and sought. A faint uncorking sound. Freed to the air his knob thrummed at my cheeks.

"Go to your room," my uncle said.

I did not look. I feared to look. I had received. I rose, legs shaking, scuffling down my dress. My bottom sucked in air and closed. Finding the door I ran down to my room.

No one came.

In my sobbing I fell asleep clothed, squeezing my bottom cheeks until oblivion came.

FIFTEEN

THE days of strangeness closed in upon us further. We were stripped and taken to the cages "to meditate," my aunt said. In my aloneness she asked me my dreams. I knelt while I told her, my face bowed. During my speaking she would allow me to raise her skirt and kiss her thighs. In such moments I was truly her slave. I buried my lips against the smooth skin above her stocking tops and licked.

"You are naturally wicked by nature," she said to me once when I had recounted a particularly vivid dream.

Maria—the maid with whom she and Katherine had toyed—stayed on. On the morning after her pleasuring she became more acquiescent and submissive to commands. Her skirts were hemmed excessively short. Whenever my uncle looked at her thighs she blushed.

One afternoon we had what my aunt called "an amusement." At lunch Maria had been complimented upon her serving of the wine and food. She looked foolishly pleased. On our retirement to the drawing room I was intrigued to see a large camera of mahogany and brass standing upon a stout tripod. Its lens faced inwards from the windows, no doubt to gather light. Before it was placed a simple wooden chair. Other furniture had been pressed back against the walls.

Upon Maria's bringing-in of the liqueurs, my aunt said to her, "Maria, we shall take your portrait today—your likeness. Will that not please you?"

Maria smiled and curtsied. "As it please you, M'am," she replied. As I learned afterwards, my uncle had rooted her with his cock the evening before, over the dining room table. She had not struggled unduly, it seemed. Katherine enlivened us by playing on the piano. It was an old melody, sad and wistful. Jenny—who had not lunched with us, having been attending to Amanda upstairs—came and joined us.

"Bring the manservant," Katherine told her.

Jenny disappeared and reappeared. There was a clattering from the distant kitchen while Maria tidied up. Once again Frederick was naked, led by his collar and chain. A blue bow was tied about the root of his penis which hung limp. Jenny led him to the chair and turned him to stand beside it, facing the camera.

Aunt Maude wiped her lips with a lace hanky and went out. A sound of scuffling came—a slap—then a silence. In a minute or two my aunt entered with Maria who wore now open-net stockings, knee boots, a tiny black corset which left her breasts and navel uncovered, and a large feathered hat such as one might see at Ascot. Her face was well adorned with powder and rouge. Her eyes were heavy-lidded.

At the sight of Frederick she started back. A loud smack on her naked bottom quickly corrected her.

"Go and sit in the chair—act as a lady—this is a formal portrait," my aunt told her. My uncle sat with his arms crossed. The wobbling of Maria's large bottom cheeks as she obeyed absorbed him. Her bush was dark—thick and luxuriant. Hot-cheeked she sat and faced us.

"Cross your legs, Maria—how dare you show yourself!" my aunt snapped at her.

Katherine lit a cigarette. The smoke coiled about us like incense.

Aunt Maude moved to the camera and bent behind it, casting a large black velvet cloth over her head and shoulders, as over the back of the camera itself. Her hand sought forward and focussed the big brass lens. Maria's eyes had a sullen look. Aunt Maude took one slide of the pair, cautioning them to be still for a full minute. Then my uncle rose and assisted her in changing the glass plates.

"Raise your right hand, Maria, and let his prick lie on your palm!" Katherine said.

There was hesitation. Imperceptibly Frederick's prick stirred and thickened as it lay on Maria's warm, moist hand. Maria would have bitten her lip in dismay if my aunt had not told her sharply to keep her expression fixed in a smile.

With small variations Aunt Maude continued photographing. The light was excellent, she observed. By the fourth attempt Frederick's prick stemmed fully upright, the flesh swelling around and above the neat blue bow. Maria was forced to hold it now. Her face had a dull, vapid look.

"It is done " Aunt Maude said at last. She collected the heavy glass plates together. They would be framed in gilt, she said.

"I will take them now," Katherine said. Walking across to Frederick whose penis had not lost its fine erection, she took hold of his chain. "Get up," she said quietly to Maria. She smiled across at me. Did she know I wanted her?

"Where shall you take them?" Aunt Maude asked.

"To the stable. It is time they were coupled." A short squeal came from Maria as Katherine moved behind her and inserted a finger upwards between the globing cheeks of her bottom. "So tight and plump—she will milk him deeply," she smiled. Her smile had a taste of olives.

Maria jerked forward and went to kneel at my aunt's feet. "M'am, I beg you!" she pleaded.

Katherine clicked her fingers and Jenny came forward with a leather neckband and chain which she secured quickly around Maria's neck.

My aunt's eyes were kindly. She gazed down at the top of Maria's bent head.

"Beg me you should, Maria. What a foolish woman you are." Her hands raised her skirt. The dark vee of her pubis was apparent to all our eyes through her white, split drawers. Her bared thighs came warm and sleek to Maria's face. Maria lifted her head slowly. Her tongue emerged, mouth hovering about the plump mound whose curls sprouted so thickly. The lips moved against her lips. My aunt's legs spread a little. Maria's tongue made a broad wet smudge around her pouting.

"Rise now!" my aunt said to her. The chain clinked. Jenny pulled on it and drew the woman to her feet.

"M'am. . . ." Maria's lips quivered. She looked like an overgrown girl who did not know what to do. Her nipples protruded thickly on her large, milky breasts. The surrounding circles were broad, crinkly. The flesh was firm.

"You will obey, Maria. Mare and stallion in the stable—it is fitting. Go now!" Aunt Maude ordained.

Katherine led them out. Through the windows I could see the trio crossing lawn towards the paddock.

Aunt Maude turned to us. "Go upstairs," she said, "you should not have watched."

In my room I made to remove my dress. We were never permitted in our bedrooms to remained clothed. Frequently now we were inspected. The hairs of my mount were occasionally trimmed to form a neat line below my navel. It would make the rest of my curls cluster more thickly, Katherine had said. She entered as I drew my dress up to my waist in preparation for removing it. Without halting her pace she stepped quickly forward and cupped the naked cheeks I exposed. I wriggled immediately to her fondling touch.

"Do you want to go to the water closet?" she asked. I nodded. I had drunk much wine. "And I—come with me."

The water closet had been newly installed. There were not then many in use. The annex in which it stood was large. A mirror was fastened to the door which faced the white and blue-flowered basin. Leading within and bidding me to lock the door, Katherine immediately raised her dress and squatted.

"Hold me—hold me while I do it," she murmured.

I held back. I hesitated, but she seized my wrist and drew my hand between her thighs. The hairs of her sex around the pouting lips tickled my fingers. A murmur escaped her mouth that I recognised as one of deep pleasure. I felt her moistness, the oily slit. Her arm came up and drew my face down. Our mouths merged in a misty sweetness. My senses swam. Impulsively I cupped her furred treasure which of a sudden gushed out a fine golden rain over my palm as her tongue intruded into my mouth. Its long wet coiling around my own tongue together with the warm flooding over my hand hypnotised me. She gripped my wrists until the last trickle.

"You now—you do it," she said.

I protested weakly. Rising, she moved me around and raised my dress. My bottom was presented to the bowl. My knees trembled. I loosed my waiting flow in turn, drenching her palm and fingers while we kissed. She held me until the last seepings. Then we dipped our hands into a bowl of water and dried them on a thin towel that hung on a nail.

Emerging, Katherine laid a hand on my shoulder. "Your uncle wishes now to see you," she said. "He waits in his study."

I had not visited the sanctum before. My footsteps along the passageway slowed. Katherine's hand pressed lightly against the small of my back. "Do not be wilful," she urged. The kaleidoscope of my thoughts spun. The moment we entered, my uncle's arms engaged me. I pulsed in his arms like a small bird taken in the hand.

"Has she been good?" he asked of Katherine over my shoulder. A laugh came from her. A sprinkling of falling silver leaves.

"She wet my hand in the closet," Katherine said, "her thighs are wet still. Feel her."

Moving swiftly up behind me she raised my dress clear to my hips, then caught my arms and drew them tightly behind me.

"Open your legs and show him. See—the damp is still on her thighs," she said. My face was scarlet. I writhed helplessly in her grasp while my uncle surveyed me at his leisure, the slimness of my calves, upswelling of thighs, the trimness of curls where my treasure was entrapped. White of belly.

Of a sudden then I was flung against him. His prodder, hidden by his breeches, stung my thigh. In his bear hug I was lifted, swung. The edge of a waiting couch came against the backs of his knees. In falling he drew me with a simple motion over his lap, my jellied breasts exposed in turn by the upwreathing of my dress.

"No, Uncle, no!"

My gasp came in the upsweeping of his hand which blasted down on to my naked bottom.

I yelped, I cried. The burning was immense.

"No, no, no, NO!" I sobbed again. My training had left me. Fire blazed in my cheeks. My legs kicked. I clawed at the carpet. The splatting of his palm came down again and again. I was woman and child. My bottom reared and flamed. Pearls of tears cascaded down my cheeks.

"*Ya-aaaah!*" I screeched again and again until he stopped and I lay limp, helpless to his caressing. The big palm glossed my globe, his fingers delved. I burbled out my sorrows. His free hand sought my dangling gourds.

"Get up, Beatrice!" Katherine intoned.

Blear-eyed and wriggling like a fish I came upright. Her arms clasped my waist tightly, allowing the insensate wriggling of my bottom to continue. Her mouth sought mine. I choked. Salt tears were at my lips. Her voice coaxed me, murmuring upon my mouth, breath to breath. A haze of wine and perfume. She had raised her dress. Our stocking tops rubbed together. The cream of my bubbling bubbled to her lips. Cunningly she parted her legs, rubbing her slit against mine, her hold not lessening about me.

"How oily your quim—how stiff your nipples, sweet."

I gulped her words within my mouth. Wildly they swam, my head invading. Gulping to pulping of lips and tongues. Hot tongues in my bottom licked my groove. Long she held me, coaxing, kissing. My torso shimmered. A stickiness between our bellies grew—a mist of perspiration. In silence my uncle sat behind me waiting.

The stinging in my bottom eased, became a throbbing. Lost in time and space I stood. Her mouth was my haven. A strange torpor seized me. I felt my legs parted until I stood straddled. Katherine's fingertips quested my globe, parted its cheeks.

"Let him see—let him see, Beatrice. He has stilled you, has he not—after your whipping?"

"St . . . st . . . st. . . ." I stuttered. Her fingers clawed the opening of my cheeks. She held me but loosely. An insolence of power.

"Stilled, yes, Beatrice. His rod in your bottom. A single plunge within. We call it that. Move backwards now. Move slowly, inch by inch."

In the cobwebs in the corners were there words? Released, my hands caught empty air, fastened upon the wraiths of yesterdays. With a small shriek I fell upon my uncle's lap. Exposed, his penis upthrust 'twixt my thighs. My bottom churned, uplifted, fell—the velvety knob of his penis-prober against my belly.

I bounced, I burbled, twisted and was held. Then Katherine bent over me. My chin upraised. I felt him jerk. Her working fingers round his penis worked. Her knuckles grazed my belly in his working. Her eyes were laughter. Her hand moved faster. His hands beneath my armpits weighed my breasts. The bud of my slit swelled, my rosy clitty. His balls chattered against my bottom. A finger sought my nest and rubbed.

My uncle groaned. His teeth bit lightly into my shoulder. His palms burnished my stiffened nipples. I felt his loins move in their strength. Of a sudden, thick jets of sperm spattered my belly. I melted, died. I moistened his balls in my spending. My breasts swelled. My belly was wet with his come. The last drops sprinkled. I swayed back to his swaying, legs apart.

"Go," Katherine said. She pulled me up, my dress high-wreathed. The door mouth opened, swallowed me. There was a sound of kissing behind me.

His come dried quickly on my skin. Some had spattered the tops of my stockings. There was quiet in the house as always, as if everyone had left. From the landing window I looked out upon the lawn and saw Caroline lying on the grass. Jenny was kissing her.

I lay down on my bed. The ceiling darkened and lowered until it enfolded me.

I ran through caverns and saw magic lights.

SIXTEEN

AUNT MAUDE wakened me in my early morning warmth. She brought me tea. I sat up and drank from a translucent cup.

"You were bad yesterday—do you know you were bad?" she asked. She fondled my hair while I drank. I did not know what to answer. Often in those days I did not know.

My aunt drew down the sheet and tutted. "Your stockings are laddered," she said. I had not bothered to take them off. She rose and took new ones from a drawer. The sheet was laid down to the end of the bed. Caressing my legs she drew off my stockings and replaced them. The new, black ones were of openwork style that came to the very tops of my thighs. "It is better so," she said and waited until I had finished the tea.

"You will be a good girl now, Beatrice, will you?"

I said yes with my eyes. My eyes were soft with the morning. My aunt removed my nightdress and attended to my face with powder and rouge.

"Maria was bad—do you remember?" she asked.

I said yes. My voice was soft with the morning. It was yesterday or the day before. I had forgotten the day.

"Amanda improves a little. Arabella is properly settled now of course," Aunt Maude continued. She glossed my long hair with a brush. Its bristles tickled my back. "They are not as you are, Beatrice. Turn over now—your bottom up, well up."

I obeyed. I drew my knees up. I was to be punished for my wickedness in the water closet and the study. My wrists were strapped to the sides of the beds where the iron supports ran beneath the mattress. Then my ankles.

"Dip your back properly—present yourself, Beatrice!" Her tone was sharp. When I did, she moved back behind me. I laid my cheek on the pillow and waited. "Such a perfect bottom—you surpass us all," she breathed.

The whip was in her hand, taken from beneath my pillow. The thongs flicked out, making me arch and rear like a filly. I turned my face inwards and bit into my pillow. The tips stung and searched me—messengers of seeking. They sought my crevices. Their small mouths nipped and made me writhe. Heat expanded. Tendrils of fire—hot in their seeking. The hissing hissed to my bold cheeks, my pumpkin, skirting my offered fig, my honeypot. Much as I squirmed and gasped the sensation had its bitter sweetness. The straps held me.

A sound beyond. The whip fell. My face rustled in its hiding in the pillow. My uncle entered. I knew his steps, the heavy footsteps falling. I struggled at my straps. My hips weaved. My eyes closed, opened, closed. The bed sagged between my legs—my legs splayed wide.

"No, Uncle, No!"

"Be quiet, Beatrice!" Her hand stroked my hair. "Slap her hard, Thomas, if she wriggles. She must learn!"

I gargled, gurgled, squealed. Thong-kissed, my cheeks were parted. The knob of his wicked nosed against my O, the puckered rim. Hands clasped my hips and stilled their wayward motions. The rim yielded. I received an inch of throbbing shaft. I endeavoured to tighten. Too late. The piston pistoned. Half his cock was sheathed.

"How tight she grips!" he groaned. Subtle and smooth he urged it more within. "What a bottom of glory—hot hot, how clinging! Your tongue, Maude!"

I heard their lips, the licking. Her hand slipped beneath my belly, fondled the lips of my quim and parted them, seeking my clit. I bucked. The movement allowed my uncle's prick to bury itself farther. Their lips sucked apart. I moaned in my writhings, in his steely grip.

"*Aaaaah!*" I gasped, my breath expelled. Without warning he had lodged it full within. The long thick prick throbbed deep within my bottom. Leaning over me, his palms cupped my swaying breasts.

My aunt moved back, forcing her way beneath me where I knelt. My head swam. My moistening anus held its velvet grip. Half-emerging, his tool sheathed itself to the full again, emerged, and then repeated the gesture. Sparks sprinkled in my belly. My hot cheeks churned against his form.

Aunt Maude drew my mouth down upon her own.

"Move your bottom, Beatrice—move it on his cock."

I blubbered in her mouth. Her tongue lapped my seepings. Moving more easily now his stiff penis commenced its majestic indriving. I jolted with his jolts. A sharp tingling sweetness in my slit increased.

"Move your bottom—you are on the rocking horse—pretend."

Coarse in her excitement, my aunt clasped my cheeks. Our mouths were sucking sponges together. I lapped as greedily as she. I moved my hips. An insensate lust seized me to feel his spurting. Lewdly I churned my bottom, drawing hoarse cries of delight from my uncle whose cock pistoned me ever faster. His hands caressed my stockinged thighs. They joined with my aunt's in fondling my breasts.

"Yes!"

In my aunt's mouth I moaned my lostness.

"Make him come in your bottom, Beatrice."

"Yes!"

"Do you not know your power, my love? Ram his belly—empty his balls!"

The words . . . were they the words . . . the power? I moved, I choked, my senses swirled. My tongue in my aunt's mouth, I drew the cheeks of my bottom forward until I could almost feel the knob at my rim.

"Hold now!" Aunt Maude instructed. She had slid from beneath me and joined her husband. I squeezed upon the knob which like a plum was lodged just within. "Be still, Thomas!" I heard, "Beatrice, you will move at your wish now."

Head hung, my lips pursed tight beyond her seeing. A final test of my total obedience? The leaves of old albums turned their pages slowly in my mind. My teeth chattered briefly. The lure was now exquisite. Unmoving as my uncle was in his stillness, I urged back. A certain oiliness between us had eased the passage. My bottom expanded comfortably but tightly round his tool. I heard his breathing come more coarsely as inch by inch I absorbed it to the full.

"No movement, Thomas," my aunt breathed. A small husky sob escaped me. I began to jerk my bottom in little frenetic stabs. Each one allowed me to feel the full length of his pestle. The rubbery rim of my anus mouthed it more tightly. I could accomodate my pressure, as it seemed.

"At your own pace, Beatrice. Are you coming?"

I could scarce breathe for the excitement of sensations. The feeling was unique. The heat in my bottom added to the wicked, itchy-burning of my submission. The pressure of my cheeks to his belly in the slow backward strokes had an intimacy all its own.

I had come twice in far-faint thrilling spillings. Lifting my head slightly, I rotated my bottom with his cock half lodged within me. His croaks were my reward. The urgent throbbings of his tool redoubled.

"You wish him to come, Beatrice?"

I did not understand. Why was I asked? Who then was master here? His hands no longer held my hips. Each movement was of my own volition.

"Y . . y . . . yes," I stammered. My voice was a small girl voice. Sunlight in the attic, hazed with dust. The stone cooler where the wine had waited in our aftermaths. The wrigglings of my bottom as I descended the ladder, my mouth clouded with summer.

I heard a gasp from my uncle. His statuesque pose astonished—the root of his manhood unmoving as I urged upon its lusts. A deep quivering seized him in the next soft smacking of my bottom to his belly. The mouth of my O gripped him as in a velvet vice. As of an instinct I held my plump cheeks now tight into him and squirmed. His groans resounded. Ah! the jetting, the deep liquid in-spurts—each long thick pulsing of come known, felt, absorbed in spongelike warmth. I sniffled, tightened, hissed my breath.

The globs shot out again, insucked. My anus flowed with riches, trickling out.

Swimming in sensations, I collapsed. The slug of flesh plopped out—wet nose upon my thighs. My bonds were loosed. A shuffling from behind and he was gone, seed spent, the sac of his balls lighter.

Drowsy in my sweet fulfilments I was turned. I lay upon my back. Her mouth touched mine. Fingers felt my wetness both at my mound and my bottom.

"It is good," Aunt Maude murmured. My body fluttered and trembled still. My thighs lay open, wanton. Our tongues touched. My lips were petals to her stamen-seeking. My aunt turned the pages in my mind and read from them silently, slowly.

"What do you want?" she asked.

I sought a word. "Everything," I said. The word was a butterfly caught in a net. Its wings were unbroken. Her eyes released it again. It flew about us and melted within me. Her finger traced my lower lip, causing me to pout. Without meaning to I giggled.

"Jenny is in a cage," my aunt said.

I did not believe her. For a moment I did not believe her. I tightened my thighs together but she tickled me and made them lie wide again, my legs straight in their net stockings.

"Dress now. Wear drawers. Be firm with her. Tell her what you would have her do."

In my rising I stared at her. The room yawned about me. I fussed with my dress. Oozings of sperm slide-slithered down my thighs at the back.

"It is true?" I asked.

Aunt Maude laughed and lifted my chin. "Why else were you sent? Do you not know yet your beginnings and your endings? Have you not been nurtured, led to this? Their cocks would have been your undoing. Would you be as Caroline, Amanda, or Jenny?"

My head would not move. I was rigid in my knowings.

"Even so, there may be lewdnesses—at your permitting. Your freedom is entire now, Beatrice. I shall mark your progress. Instill, train, command. Do you understand?" She loosed my chin. I nodded. The air about my eyes had lost its mist. The sperm had bubbled from Caroline's bottom, perhaps, long ere this. I made appraisals, promisings—within myself I delved and sought. The cheeks of my bottom were heavy, warm, fulfilled.

I turned from her and made my way upstairs. The door to my uncle's study lay open. He was writing at his desk. At my passing he looked up. His eyes were hollow. I swayed my hips with a certain insolence. I wished him to look. "How firm and fleshy you are," my aunt had said. I sensed my perversities. The air of the house hung now about me like an old cloak.

Jenny was naked in a cage. Amanda lay upon the couch on her back, tightly bound from head to feet. I unlocked the cage. Jenny's arms were strapped to her sides. She wore black stockings and a long string of pearls which hung between her melon breasts. She was sitting. She stared at me dully. I motioned my head and she rose with an effort, rolling for a moment against the bars. Then she recovered herself and stepped out.

I led her to the bar. I intended to strap her. Her small, tight bottom had a fascination for me. It was like Amanda's except that Jenny was shorter than she. Her hair had been trimmed in an urchin cut.

"Do not speak until I speak," I said. I bent her over the bar and gave her bottom a sharp smack. With her arms bound, it was needful for me only to touch the back of her downbent head lightly. The sound of the smack coupled with the resilience of the cheeks and the wild little gasp that she uttered thrilled me tremendously. Slowly I left her and walked over to the wall where the straps hung. I selected the shortest and thickest. Amanda's eyes beseeched me briefly. I gave her a small tight smile that betokened nothing.

"When we were younger, did Father have you?" I asked Jenny. In uttering my words I brought the leather across her bottom with a loud *Cra-aaaaack!* Her hips swayed and jerked inwards so far as the bar would allow them to. A dull flush spread across her hemispheres.

"You intend not to answer, Jenny?"

Her face was suffused. A second, sharper stroke of the leather made her yelp more.

"Yes, Beatrice."

"When you came to sleep in the guest-room?" The double doors of the past opened more clearly to me now. They yawned upon our yesterdays.

"Yesssssss!" she hissed as the loud-smacking strap again seared her bottom.

"You will tell me later in precise detail. Rise!"

Her face contorted as she did so. She swivelled round on her heels and stood before me. Her head hung. I smiled and tweaked her nipples.

"How delicious you must have been for him," I said coldly. I felt no emotion. It was an observation. I led her downstairs by her string of pearls which I knew she would fear to have broken. Her small feet padded silently on the carpet. Leading her into my room which was empty again, I gave her a further smack, making her jump. She skittered nervously forward and then stood still.

"Kneel!" I told her. A sense of severity entered into me, but I was as yet not entirely tutored. A few months hence and I would have handled her even better. Kneeling and with her head and shoulders bowed dutifully, she looked as one seeking protection. It was part of her attraction. I wanted her tongue—her small darting tongue—but it was too soon as yet.

I walked round her, inspecting her slowly. She had grown little through the years, I thought. Her body was small, curves tight and sweet.

"You were strapped that night?" I asked.

"Yes."

The little word upon the carpet lay. I stood before her once more and raised my foot, bringing the sole of my boot down gently on the back of her head. Her lips touched the toe of my other boot and kissed it.

"Begin, Jenny."

Her mouth mumbled against my boot. Her lips smudged its glossy surface. I edited her text in my mind as she spoke, sensing her slyness. Her conversion that night had been swift, as she would have had me believe. In the double bed to which she had been carried while supposedly half asleep, her nightgown had been stripped, her bottom poised. Fearful to cry out lest she woke me, the strap had scorched her. Confessions had been drawn from her that she said were false. After a score of strokes she had been stilled, even as my uncle had stilled me with a long deep plunge and then withdrawal. But then it had entered her again and so remained, deep in its throbbings.

On being carried back at last to the guest room, she had felt isolated, lonely. The silence of the house at night had hung about her like bat's wings. Her bottom knew heat and emptiness and longing. In her tinglings she had lain.

"Go on," I said when, at this part of her narrative, she halted.

"There was no more," she mumbled. Her mouth moved over my boot even more fervently.

"Do you believe her?" It was my aunt. She had entered

unseen, unheard. Her look ignored Jenny. She came across, lifted my chin and kissed me. The kiss endured. My aunt's hand reached down and sought Jenny's hair while our mouths were locked. She drew Jenny's face upwards, beneath my skirt, between my thighs. Open, warm and seeking, Jenny's lips nuzzled into the vee of my drawers. I felt the pleading lapping of her tongue. I did not move. My hips were unresponsive as if by instinct. By placing her free hand beneath my bottom, Aunt Maude could tell it was so. Her lips moved with pleasure upon mine. Our salivas mingled.

"Do you believe her?" she asked again.

I would not answer. I wanted what I knew within myself. My bottom squeezed in my remembering. My aunt's mouth swam back from mine. "Tell her," she said quietly.

I looked down. The front of my skirt was looped over Jenny's head. Her tongue worked industriously, tracing the lips of my quim through my drawers. Despite a faint trembling of my knees I moved not.

"Down!" I commanded. The surge of power was within me. I knew the power. Jenny's response was instant. She sank down again. Her mouth deserted me. "Go! go to your cage!" I said. With the closing of the door my aunt took my hand and guided me to sit upon the bed. Going to my closet she poured a liqueur for each of us. Returning, she sat beside me.

"You will continue your meditations," she said, "plan your plottings, manouevre them to your will."

The freshness of cool water was within me after my handling of Jenny.

"All?" I asked.

Aunt Maude did not answer me directly. "You dealt well with Jenny. It shall be so with Caroline and—upon your need—with Katherine. Observe the males. How proudly their cocks rise. Hidden sometimes beneath their breeches—at others lewdly exposed. Frig them, toy with them, play with them. The bubbling jets expel. Their faces soften, their cocks soften. They are as putty. Their training is no more arduous than that of the girls. They shall service you only at your bidding."

"Service?" I sensed the meaning, yet I asked.

"In your lewdnesses, Beatrice—your slit, your bottom. Never your mouth. Mouths are for others."

"Such as Caroline?"

"Sly in her sweetness, she has sucked upon their bubblings, yes. Had you not known this? She is shy, acquiescent. Her mouth lends itself like a rose to the sperm, imbibing deeply. In her demureness she wipes her lips secretively and blushes. Did you not know."

I hid my face. It was my last shyness. "Perhaps," I said. Spiders' webs glistened in my mind, broke, fell apart. I envied her for a moment—the big knob purplish at her lips, her tongue gliding beneath the veins. The urgent gliding, sliding. The silence save for the sucking of her lips. Sweet throbbing of the tool—its jets outspurting. Mouth salty, creamed, her limp form raised. Her bottom fondled.

I came to myself again. "Shall we return soon?" I asked.

"At your wish, Beatrice." A last flourish of her glass and she was gone. I leaned back. The wall was cool to my back. In the summer I would have cages on the lawn—between the shrubbery and the summerhouse. I would have my whip. My eyes would be as fire, my breasts uplifted.

Yes.

SEVENTEEN

THE letter I had begun to Father lay as I had left it. I imagined him in his being entering and gazing at it. The Chinese, I have heard, never destroy a piece of paper once it has been written upon. Characters once imparted to it acquire a being, a magic, a presence. They rest upon the surface like the silhouettes of birds who have no wish to move again.

I took up the pen again. *Dearest Father, I await your return—Beatrice*. It was enough. Now in my subtle shifting it sufficed. He would move among the words at night as a poacher moves among the larches and the elms. Taking an envelope, I addressed it to him at the tea plantation in Malabar which his father had bequeathed him. He would return from thence with dust on his lapels—the musk of dusky women in his nostrils, the dream of a rocking horse.

I would place the horse on the lawn, perhaps, in a larger cage for Caroline. When the rain came it would stand forlorn and waiting. Raindrops in their crystal glittering on its stirrups.

I bathed and listened to a twittering of voices from the garden—Caroline's and Jenny's among them. Upon my descent for lunch I employed subtleties rather than assertions. At the serving of the soup I asked Maria what wine we were to have with the fish.

"With the fish, Riesling . . ." Maria began and looked as if towards Katherine, my aunt being seemingly deeply engaged with the unfolding of her napkin.

"Not the Riesling—we will have Piesporter, Maria, and you will address me as M'am. You understand?"

The poor woman almost curtsied in her confusion whereat Katherine swept a look along the table to Aunt Maude whose placid quietness gave full reply. I had additionally had Amanda brought down. She sat as one who is at a party without friends. Katherine's look passed to me. I received it briefly with a slight affectation of boredom.

"Caroline, you will gather flowers from the garden after lunch. The rooms have a slightly drab air. Place some in my bedroom first. Amanda will assist you," I said, and turned immediately to engage my aunt in conversation. Katherine was thus neatly isolated, my uncle having gone—or been sent, I suspected—on some errand.

I rose first from the table. Normally, in the conventions, Aunt Maude would have done so and I would have waited upon her to do so. By this small sign, however, a silent Katherine received my further tokens. When I moved of a purpose into the conservatory she followed me—a slightly wounded falcon, I felt, though I bore her no malice. To the contrary, she attracted me both physically and mentally.

"There is change, then," she asked quietly.

"As to all things," I replied. I placed my arm about her waist and then slid my hand down very slowly to feel and fondle the quite perfect globe of her bottom. Beneath the light material of her dress the twin hemispheres had the smoothness of peach-skin.

Katherine compressed her lips slightly and endeavoured to hide a smile of pleasure at the lightly-floating questing of my fingers. That she wore no drawers was evident by the way I could gently urge a single fold of her dress into the tight groove of her bottom.

"You have not yet given us a performance, Katherine."

"No?" Her voice was light but shaky. She endeavoured to recover her usual poise and move away but a warning inward pressure of my fingers stayed her. "The subject was forgotten," she said. The faintest of blushes had appeared on her cheeks. It pleased me.

I drew her to a small bench where we sat side by side. The scent of fuchsias was rich in my nostrils. Earth smell, loam smell—a nostalgia of flowerpots, some straight, some tilted.

"Your performances have been few? I mean for your private theatricals, Katherine."

"Le Theatre Erotique? There have been some amusements in the past. I engaged Lord Eridge's three daughters upon a delicious masquerade last summer. It made excellent preliminary training for them. It is extraordinary what licences the erstwhile modest permit themselves when they believe themselves inhabiting a world of fantasy."

"Wherein they also believe themselves full hid by their costumes?" I asked.

Katherine's look of appraisal would have been flattering in any other circumstances.

"Exactly. They had not so much as raised their skirts before nor shown their ankles. I had them attired at first in glittering tights with knee-boots and transparent bodices. Music entranced them to display themselves. A small orchestra was discreetly screened from the proceedings. We acted out at first an innocent game of circuses. The estate ponies were perfect for that. We used a large marquee. The audience was naturally small and the champagne flowed. I allowed the girls to imbibe freely between their frolics. In their gigglings and foolish ridings around on the ponies I gave them several twitches of the crop to enervate them."

I laid my hand upon Katherine's thigh and fingered up the material of her dress slowly until her nearest leg was bared to me almost to her hip. My fingertips ran sensuously around her stocking top. She leaned back. Her lips remained slightly parted for a moment as if seeking breath. The transition from stocking top to silk-smooth skin was delicious.

"And the entertainment?" I asked. I guessed it was called that from my aunt's photographic interlude with Maria and Frederick.

"There was to be trick riding, I told them," Katherine continued. She moved her knees wider apart to allow my hand to glide up more easily and fondle the warm inner surfaces of her thighs. "The ponies were exchanged for three fine Arabian horses from Lord Eridge's stables. The door to the marquee was then tightly closed. The musicians, being in a separate marquee that abutted our own, could see nothing.

"I blindfolded each of the girls and had them mount the steeds, whereat their arms were secured about the horses' necks. There was a little fretting on their part about this, for fear they would fall. I comforted them," Katherine went on with a smile and a half-closing of her eyes as I delicately touched the lips of her quim. Her bottom shifted forward slightly on the seat.

"You strapped their ankles to the stirrups—yes, go on," I said confidently.

"First I had them ride in a circle. Unknown to them three of the menfolk guided the stallions by their reins. The sisters thought themselves most adept and laughed shrilly, if sometimes nervously. Occasionally I gave them a harder twitching with a schooling whip than they had before received. By then they were quite flushed with all the excitement. I judged them ready. The horses were stilled and to multiple shrieks from the three lovely heroines of the piece their tights were swiftly drawn down. Then with a single bound a male leapt up behind each of them, raised their bare bottoms from off the saddles and . . ."

I leaned to her. Our lips, tongues met. My forefinger circled the increasing sticky lips of her slit.

"Each was fucked more than once?" I asked. I had not intended to use a word of such coarseness. It spilled unbidden from my lips. Katherine's tongue swam around my own.

"In succession from the males —who had long waited upon such an occasion—each girl received a triple dose. They had quietened considerably by the time a second foaming lance entered their pussies. The gentle jogging of the horses as they continued to move round slowly in a circle added to their pleasures, no doubt."

"Their bottoms were feted, too?" I asked. Katherine's parted legs had straightened. I sought right beneath the sweet orb of her bottom and found her puckered rose.

"No . . . n . . . no. . . . not then," she stammered. "That pleasure had been reserved. Half fainting with untold pleasures, the girls were finally dismounted and taken blindfolded into the house, their wrists secured, their tights removed as well as their boots. Their naked bottoms were quite rosy after their ridings, of course. In the main bedroom of the manor all had been prepared beforehand. Taken within, the three were strapped side by side upon the bed with pillows piled tightly beneath their bellies to elevate their bottoms.

"The squire—entering then ready for the fray with his penis bobbing—exerted his efforts valiantly in each of their bottoms in turn, stilling each while they moaned and squirmed fretfully. Then, taking the elder—whom I placed in the middle—he pumped her bottom fully, fondling the other two meanwhile. Such was his pleasure that the rosehole—from which he finally withdrew—frothed most fully, I can tell you. Oh! oh, Beatrice—your tongue, dearest, I implore you!"

Her beseeching for my mouth between her elegant thighs was to my satisfaction since I intended then to ignore it. She had asked and been refused. It suited me perfectly. Taking her chin I pushed her face back and ceased the toying of my fingers.

"Later, perhaps," I purred, "upon your continued good behaviour. You have not finished your recital. What then occurred?"

"His prick considerably limper, of course, he left the squirming and blindfolded beauties to their wonderings as to the possesor of the doughty staff which had cleft their bottoms—not entirely to their dissatisfaction, as it later transpired. They were then released, bathed and cossetted—by myself and Jenny, as it happened. We said nothing of the lewdnesses to which they had succumbed and indeed brought wine and cakes and made merry as if the afternoon had been nought but gaiety."

"Their training began thereafter, Katherine?" My hand held her chin still in a commanding pose.

"Yes. They were clothed henceforth as you have been —in close-fitting wool dresses with nothing beneath save their stockings and boots or shoes. Frequent but light applications of the birch did wonders. With sisters—they were sixteen, eighteen and twenty respectively—it is best to keep them herded close at all times. The breakfast room, being large, was transformed into a recreation room for them. To a large circular table I had a short centre post fixed. Each girl was spread across the table with her wrists secured to the post. Their ankles were tied by a rope which circled the table and looped around their outstretched legs.

"For the first week they continued to be blindfolded when brought down, their dresses secured up around their waists. Into the breakfast room I patted them, one by one. They had adorable bottoms and were quite quiet and obedient when secured in a circle around the table. A dozen swishes of the birch came first, bringing a pink glow to their offered bottoms. The twelfth stroke was always the sternest, bringing loud shrill squeals—for they quickly learned that it was followed by the stiff insertion of the throbbing staff into each of their bottoms.

"At the end of the first week, immediately after each had been birched, I released Samantha, the eldest, while leaving the other two bound. Cautioning her to be silent, I bound her wrists and removed her blindfold. Blushing violently, she made to turn away from the upright majesty of the cock that awaited her, but I twisted her about to face it."

"You made her ask for it," I murmured.

"Of course."

Katherine's voice was husky, her eyes wild with pleading for the attentions of my tongue.

"How crude," I said softly and rose, looking down at her.

"Katherine, draw your skirt up fully—well beneath your bottom. Good. Spread your legs more. Excellent! A delicious thatch, my sweet. Has it been watered of late?"

Before she could reply I strode to the door and gazed back at her. She looked indeed a picture of wantonness, her breasts heaving. The tint of her thighs above her stockings was as of pale ivory. The bush of her quim was thick and luxuriant.

"*Wait!*" I said coldly, quickly removing the key from the door and turning it on the other side as I went out. Unmoving she sat, the beseeching of her eyes following me.

I hastened to Aunt Maude and told her of my immediate intentions. Her eyes glowed. "I will have him made ready," she said, "it will take but a moment." Summoning Maria, she told her to fetch Frederick without delay. He came as usual in his quietness—a watchfulness, I felt, that was well concealed behind a long-practised subservience.

"You will strip," I said. He gazed at me for a long moment as if uncertain as to whether he was to obey or not and then immediately removed his jacket. Assuring myself that there were no other servants about, I then fetched a simple, straight-backed wooden chair which I placed for him.

In his nakedness, Frederick was a magnificent animal, perfect in physique. His cock stood a proud nine inches under the gentle manipulation of my fingers. Bidding him sit, I then had my aunt bind him tightly to the chair facing the doors.

"You will see now to Katherine?" I asked my aunt who nodded and went out. The very mention of his mistress's name made Frederick start—not out of apprehension, I perceived, for while a dull flush spread over his cleancut features, the rubicund knob of his penis appeared to glow even more.

A scuffling sounded from beyond. I strode to the doors and opened them. There stood Katherine, wriggling in the stronger embrace of my aunt. Between us we hustled her within and closed the doors anew upon the little ceremony I intended.

"Oh how dare you!" Katherine blustered, her colour rising high at the sight of her manservant whose up-quivering tool awaited her pleasure. There was no need to remove her dress. It hoisted cleanly and swiftly enough again to her hips. While Aunt Maude held her wrists I smacked her bottom hard, causing her hips to jolt and bringing a light sheen of tears into her eyes.

"*Quiet*, Katherine!" I instructed coldly. "Has he not had you yet?" With every word her enforced but dragging footsteps brought the superb nudity of the lower half of her body closer to the manservant's haggard gaze. "No!" she shrieked. Her head shook wildly.

"You will speak!" I told him. "Have you not savoured the voluptuous pleasures of her bottom, the wobbling of her lovely breasts to your lips?"

"M . . . M'am? N . . . no. She has brought me frequently to dress her and undress her—to prepare her often for her bath—but never have my fingers been permitted to touch her adorable skin," he stammered.

Perhaps it was his unexpected use—indeed unheard of use for a servant—of the word "adorable" that brought a softer shriek than I had imagined would come, as Katherine was manouevred over him, legs apart, until his manly tool prodded up in waiting just beneath the pouting lips of her quim.

"Oh! Maude! Beatrice! I beg you—no!" Katherine sobbed in what I felt was entirely theatrical effect. No doubt in her early training of the Eridge daughters she had heard them all say it in turn. Drawing Katherine's arms forward over Frederick's shoulders, my aunt continued to hold her while I—pressing my hand downwards upon her bottom —reached beneath and guided the stiff cock of a now groaning Frederick between the soft lips of her slit.

Katherine's eyes rolled. Her head fell back, her knees trembling on either side of his as the nubbing nose of his lovestaff urged within her luscious grotto and secured its place. The rest was but a matter of a simple downward thrust on Katherine's shoulders. A low humming sound which appeared to mingle shock and pleasure trilled from her throat as her brazen bottom cheeks at last descended upon Frederick's bare knees, there to settle with a squirming, agonised motion.

The rest was simplicity. In a trice she was bound to him, the bodice of her dress being unlaced so that his nose settled somewhat blissfully no doubt in the deep valley between the silken gourds of her tits.

Dearly as I would have loved to have knelt down, I did not. It would have been undignified. Nevertheless, I would like to have seen—on that first occasion—the deep rooting of his cock within her and the way his balls were squashed beneath her. Her arms were secured around his neck and her ankles fastened to his. Thus she had room to manouevre her bottom up and down and would do so, I had no doubt, once they were alone, despite her sobbing protestations as Aunt Maude and I made to leave.

"B . . . Beatrice! you cannot!" Katherine implored. Imprisoned and shafted upon him thus, she looked adorable. Her nipples already sprouted thickly, I noticed. I had no illusions that the moment we left them in this erotic stance his lips would begin nibbling at the rosy buds her exposed melons presented to him.

"You may come in her as you wish . . . on this occasion, Frederick," I said quietly. Then we were gone, the doors locked behind us.

"A merriment—did you not think?" I asked Aunt Maude.

My aunt nodded. "It will do her no harm. She has long inhibited herself in his respect, I am sure. You will not permit him to master her, though?"

It was an unnecessary question, as her eyes told me. There were permutations into which I had not yet entered nor thought to enter.

"I shall make her Mistress of the Robes," I said, and laughed. We placed our ears to the door briefly and caught their muffled moanings. "She will speak not a word to him out of pride," I said, "and neither will he dare address her despite the fact that he has her plugged. An almost perfect conjunction, I think. She may punish him later, at her wish, of course. I shall permit that. They will enjoy that also —both of them."

"You have grown in your knowings," Aunt Maude replied.

"Of course," I said pertly. The exercise had given me a heady feeling of conquering without cruelty—the path I was thereafter to follow in all my knowings. Eight persons out of ten have a willingness to submit in the right circumstances and guided by the right hands. Therein is a safety for them. They are led—permitted. In their enforcement are they permitted. I had moved beneath the sea and raised my skirts. The water had lapped me. A tongue had lapped me. Fishes had nibbled at my garters.

I would have a dozen pairs of gloves of the finest kid, reaching to my elbows, I told my aunt. The idea of the very sensuousness of their touch communicated itself to her immediately. She would have her glove-maker bring them she said. They would be extremely close-fitting.

"Their come will bubble over your fingers," she smiled.

"When I wish it," I said. "Come—I want you on the rocking horse."

Aunt Maude stepped back. "I?" She jerked, but my hand already had her elbow. "Do you mean it, Beatrice?" I had no need to answer. Her docility came as from one who had half expected it. Stockinged and booted, but otherwise naked, she looked superb. Her figure had a rubbery firmness in all its outcurving aspects. Mounted on the horse, she stretched her bottom back brazenly, her slit gleaming juicily.

I accorded her no pleasure other than three dozen biting flicks of the whip. The enforced bending of her knees—together with the orbing of her bottom—as she fought to keep her heels dug into the stirrups, provided the very aspect of eroticism I had long envisaged of myself.

There would be a small platform in future behind the horse so that the male could mount it at the appropriate moment and insert his penis while he gripped the weaving hips.

At my command.

I would have it so. There would be no exercises nor entertainments nor merriments beyond my seeing or control.

I had entered my domain.

EIGHTEEN

IT was a full forty minutes before I released Katherine and drew her up. Her nipples were rigid, her breasts swollen. Following me in with a distinctly awkward gait after the whipping I had accorded her, my aunt released Frederick and motioned him to dress in a side room.

"How many times, Katherine?" I asked softly, passing my hand down between her thighs. The abundance of his sperm made itself felt soapily between her thighs. Some had trickled down and rilled into the ridged tops of her stockings.

Burying her hot face into my shoulder, Katherine mumbled something I could not catch. It would not do. I lifted her reluctant face, watching the sly messengers of pleasure endeavouring to scurry into hiding behind her eyes.

"He came twice at least, I trust?" I asked sternly. Again she wanted to conceal her face but I would not permit it.

Katherine nodded. I had yet to learn myself that it is one of the most satisfying positions, squatted face to face upon a man's thighs. "Yes," she averred thickly. "Beatrice, I must . . ."

"Punish him? Of course—at your pleasure," I interrupted. An exceedingly pretty half laugh broke from her lips, accompanied by a small, emerging *"Oh!"* that had all the colour and perfume of a budding rose. I drew her dress down as a mother might with a child and soothed her hips.

"You will not make me again?" she asked. The invitation was so blatant that I all but laughed.

"Obedience is necessary at all times, Katherine," I replied softly and kissed her brow. It was damp still with her exertions as were her peachlike bottom cheeks which held a faint mist of moisture between them. It would have pleasured me distinctly then to have guided another man-root into her bottom while holding her down beneath my arm. Perhaps she read the wish in my eyes for she simpered and pressed into me.

"I should never . . ." she began. I knew her intention. It was to apologise to me for what had gone before. Perhaps she thought I had come in disguise to test her.

"You may have Jenny as a handmaid—for today, Katherine."

I moved away quickly and left her. She would have had me stay, I felt—perhaps to afford her some obscure sense of comforting. One must keep one's distance, however. I had turned her about neatly and left her, so to speak, with one foot in mid-air. My immediate concern was with Amanda. She had dallied long in the garden with Caroline. Nevertheless, their would-be pleasing efforts were evident from the array of blooms which stood on the kitchen table.

Maria was adjusting some of them. She gazed at me rather shyly as I entered.

"You are happy, Maria?" I asked. The bloom of health seemed indeed to be upon her. I had a certain taste for the voluptuousness of her curves which her deliberately tight and abbreviated costume enhanced. She nodded. A veil of uncertainty was in her eyes. Her fingers flustered at the flowers. There was a new ring on her finger, I noticed. It was one of no great account. My uncle had given it to her, I guessed. On my questioning her, she confessed it.

"He mounted you, Maria?"

The question was so direct that she knew not what to answer. A tiny bubble of saliva appeared between her lips which were richly curved but smallish.

"As Frederick did in the stable, Maria?" I insisted. Beneath her black skirt I could envisage the ripeness of her cheeks in their waiting.

"My husband don't know, M'am," she stammered.

"Answer the questions, Maria," I said softly and stayed her hands from their toying with the stalks of the blooms. Her palms were moist.

"I was ashamed, M'am," she choked. The expression in her eyes was ill-disguised. It followed not the twisting of her lips. She would lend herself, I sensed, to whatever I intended.

"Did you buck or struggle, Maria?" I gripped the bun of her hair which was coiled up with hairpins. One loosened and fell between my fingers.

"No, M'am, I daren't. Miss Katherine she had the whip, in the stable, and the Mistress she warned me not to move afterwards when I was in the dining room over the table."

I was but half listening. Though not indolent, she was learning her pleasures in the sly way known to such women. An occasional protest cleared her conscience, as she saw it.

Her husband, she said, was a good man, a quiet man, like herself nearing thirty. He worked as a farm labourer.

I released her hair.

"You will come shortly into my service, Maria—as also your husband. There will be work for him to do around the house. I am having a site cleared for stables. You may perhaps be my Stable Mistress, and it so please me. You have learned a little of the handling of females and you are acquiescent. You will learn under my instructions."

I doubted whether she knew the meaning of "acquiescent" any more than she would have recognised a five-pound note. I have since given field-girls a guinea piece for their intended services and seen them gaze at it in wonder.

Words unspoken danced upon Maria's lips. From the brief description she had given me of her husband, Ned, he would be amply able to service both Caroline and Jenny when required. Maria—given over to such pleasures as I occasionally permitted her—would soon grow used to it.

Amanda I called within. Lolling upon a rug on the lawn, Caroline stared at me in some wonder. I gave her a smile. "Later," I called. It would comfort her for a while. In my uprising was her safety, as she knew. The memory of being bound to her in our nudities was still one of my sweetest. We would play games of remembrance, perhaps. I would find a way. She would become my favourite handmaiden, an adored one. In the attic would be laughter again. I would brush her hair and fondle and pat her bottom, coaxing. In her shaftings would be the whisperings of sunhazed lust. The bees' wings on the windowsill would stir. I would make colours to enchant her eyes. Filled and fulfilled she would be led down the ladder again, her legs in their slimness-sweet uncovered still. The gold between her thighs would glint with sperm. In her richness.

"Is there richness, Amanda?" I asked. Knowing not, she

did not answer. There was awkwardness in her gait as I led her up. Her small, tight bottom was attended to daily and yet still it jerked skittishly at the first stroke of leather or birch.

In my bedroom I stilled Amanda with my hand and made her stand, feet together, while I sat on the bed.

"This will be your first new exercise—to stand still on command. Will you do so, Amanda, if you are no longer caged or birched?"

She nodded, an arising of hope in her eyes.

"What is it you seek?" I asked. "There will be the strap still."

"I do not know," she mumbled. In my intuitions she was a relatively poor subject, though I knew not why. Rising, I moved around her and passed my hand up beneath her skirt to see whether or not she would flinch. She did not. I urged my thumb against her rosehole. Aunt Maude inserted the dildo twice daily in her now. It had improved her, I noticed. A tiny assenting movement of her bottom made itself felt against my thumb.

"You do not mind the strap?" I asked. I moved the ball of my thumb up and down between the elastic cheeks.

Amanda shook her head in a manner that was at least uncertain. Perhaps she feared to say no—or perhaps pride held her back. There was a possibility by now that she had begun to accept it with a surprised sense of pleasure—the stinging a challenge.

"Raise your dress, Amanda, and tuck it in about your waist. Feet together, hands at sides. Good. You will stand so when you are told. It will be a further exercise. Your thighbands—should they not be of silver now? Have you earned them?"

"I have been good." Her lips quivered. Was she aware to what she had replied? I thought of the house from which we had led her here. The gloom of the rooms—the latticed windows too small. Male hands that had quavered briefly about our breasts.

"Silver," I repeated. I ran my fingers around the metal bands. "He is a jeweller, is he not? Would you not prefer silver?"

"I suppose." The dull tone of her voice had the lustreless feel of the back of a dry spoon run over the tongue.

"Then it shall be," I told her. Her eyes moved not. Could Aunt Maude have handled her differently, to a better end? I felt certain not. The curls about her pubic mount were tight and neat, trimmed straight across the top as my own had been. The curve of her belly was very slight, her breasts gelatinous and firm. I would have written messages on her mind save that in reading them she would not comprehend them. In two or three years perhaps she would be betrothed. Her eyes would move with vagueness through her days. Men would kiss her and bed her. She would respond with a vacuousness that would disappoint all save the lust-seekers.

He who was to mount her and fashion the broad rings of silver for her thighs would be such. They were mere oddments of people—of no account. Had there at least been slyness in her I could have used it, wended it within my wendings, eased tunnels of discovery.

By seven that evening, after the despatch of Frederick as messenger, the jeweller arrived. His eyes were haggard with expectancy.

"So soon?" he asked me. His eyes held querulous dismay that I, who had permitted my breasts to be fondled by him, should now have taken charge.

"Amanda waits upstairs," I replied. Doffing his hat and cloak he accompanied me in some evident wondering, which I uttered no words to satisfy. At the turn of the stairs that led to the caging room I halted for a moment. "It shall be as I say. You will do all that I say. You will not speak unless I request it. Otherwise a delicate balance will be disturbed. Thereafter you may take her back. You will find her acquiescent. There is but one thing more," I added, leading him in.

At the sight before him he stopped dead. Amanda was over the bar, her body freshly bathed and perfumed. I had deemed it necessary to tie her wrists so that she could not rise. Her long legs were neat together. Naked, her bottom rendered its perfect apple shape. I closed the door upon us.

"Remember my words—the fine balance," I told him again in a whisper. He accepted with a nod—deeming himself perhaps in Paradise. His eyes were tentacles about her yielded form. Aloud, I added for Amanda's benefit, "Next week her common metal thigh bands are to be replaced by silver ones. You will no doubt think of an appropriate design to engrave around them. Remove your clothes now and watch."

"R . . . r . . . remove?" he stuttered.

"Or you shall not have her. There are certain conventions that we have instilled in her," I went on glibly. The entire scene amused me not overmuch but I intended to have it performed. It was my first experiment in any event with an unconditioned male. "You agree to give her solid silver stocking bands?" I asked.

"If it is wished," he croaked. Under my waiting eyes his hands fiddled with the undoing of his waistcoat.

"It is wished," I replied.

With others the edge of farce might already have been reached, but here within this strange room and with Amanda perfectly poised for his pleasuring, the dolt was ready to accept all that I said. Her very muteness added to the occasion.

A florid cast came into his features as he commenced

with ludicrous reluctance to remove his clothes in front of me. I affected not to look at him. There was a certain brawniness in his figure which perhaps had its brutish attraction. His trunk was thick, his thighs tree trunks. At the first offering of his nakedness his penis lolled inert but rose in anticipation as I led him to her. I had oiled Amanda's bottom already in preparation for the moment. To all appearances she hung there dazed. Only a slight trembling of her knees betrayed her.

He himself appeared now as one in a trance. Placing my hand in the small of his back I urged him yet a step forward. Stemming upwards, his penis—which was of full girth and good length—pressed its pulsing column against the inrolling of her nether cheeks. Amanda immediately uttered a small cry, jerking like a nervous filly. The movement served only to bulge her bottom deeper against his balls.

"In silence, please, your wrists together behind your back," I told him.

The gaping of his mouth at these words gave him an air of great stupidity. Nevertheless he obeyed. Taking him entirely by surprise in the fretful impatience of his loins, I manacled his wrists. His face became purplish.

"Silence!" I warned, "the first act is intended as a ceremonial. You will receive instructions on how to handle her during the first weeks hereafter."

Amanda's head began to toss. She strained at her wrist bonds. The most tearful of protests escaped her. She had awoken it seemed from the lulling comfort of her bondage. I had expected it. My next act therefore surprised her since, moving around to the front of the bar where her shoulders hung, I untied her wrists.

"Do not move," I warned her. "You have your choice even so. Accept his cock in you at last or you will stay for a further three months here. Do you understand?"

"P . . . please—I don't want him to."

Her voice appeared piteous, small—of unutterable appeal. It moved me not since no upward movement of her back occurred. Some hint of slyness for which I had previously sought in vain was apparent in her at last for she gripped the bar, though nervously, and held her bottom remarkably still, her hair flowing down about her face.

I moved back to where her stallion stood, his eyes glassy with despair as—bereft of the use of his arms—he endeavored to manouevre his swollen crest against the rim of her rosehole.

"Permit me," I said and seized his rod which throbbed enormously in my palm. Motioning him back and thereby permitting him for the first time in his life no doubt the intimate attendance of two females at once, I urged his stiff shaft down and positioned the ruddy knob against Amanda's well-oiled aperture. "Enter her slowly," I breathed.

His knees trembled violently, jaw sagging, as the rubbery rim yielded with petulant moans and cries from Amanda. In but a second the knob was engulfed—the shaft itself standing proud. Its veins throbbed in their eagerness. Gripping the hairs at the back of his neck I drew upon them sharply, bringing from him a surprised groan. Sodomy—though males know it not—is an act of worship towards the superior sex. For to whatever bondage or apparent humiliations females are brought, they remain—as Aunt Maude had taught me now—the eternal victors of the act. Able as they are to receive a succession of pulsing and apparently dominant penises, it is the males who retire wan and spent.

Thus did I monitor the act. Gliding my hand between them and taking his pendent eggs in the palm of my hand, I restricted his entry half-inch by half-inch, ignoring—as I well knew I could—the anguished cries and sobbings of

Amanda and the febrile jerkings of his loins as he sought to sheathe his rod more quickly.

"*Whoooo! Whoooo! No! No-Oh! Ah!* stop him, please!" Amanda moaned endlessly. At the half mark, however, his heavy trunk had now leaned more on hers until he was all but fully bent over her, his breath raucous. I had taken his balls now from behind. The pressures of my fingers were warnings enough for him to proceed as if by stealth into the clamlike gripping of her depths.

"B . . . b . . . b . . . b . . . !" Amanda moaned incoherently. I knew the wildness of her mind—the surging of the seawaves there—the outward rushing of the breath. Her eyes bulged. For a moment her hands deserted the gripping bar below in such a gesture that I feared rebellion. Loosing his testicles I gave then his buttocks a hearty slap, the immediate result of which was to ram his root completely within her bottom.

Ah! her wild, high-pitched shriek!

"*Na-ah-aaaaaaaaah!*" she shrilled, but deeply corked as she now was, her hips were immobile, her sobs spilling down upon the blankly staring floor.

Straps, whose purpose had not signified themselves to him, came swiftly to my hands. Groaning, he felt the grinding of her bottom warm into his belly as I strapped their thighs together at the top and buckled quickly. Only the slightest movement of his loins was now possible. I could but guess at the ecstasy of sensations he was experiencing. Bound thus in the most bizarre manner, his wrists strained helplessly at the manacles, his buttocks twitching as Amanda's gripping bottom first tightened upon him and then undoubtedly relaxed.

I moved and knelt before her, raising her hot-flushed face to mine. Her eyes were half-closed, giving a pretty fluttering to the lashes. Easing my palms forward uppermost, I allowed her tits to weigh upon them. Her nipples, as I had expected, had hardened into thornlike points. Her lips lolled wet beneath my passing kiss. There was no need for speech. Her mind did not communicate itself to me.

"R . . . r . . . release!" he croaked.

I saw no need to. Her bottom needed to accomodate itself to him more fully. Leaving them in their posture, I descended and found Caroline drinking lemonade in the breakfast room. Aunt Maude had taken Jenny and Katherine out, it seemed. More immediately upon my appearance, however, Caroline rose and threw herself into my arms.

"May we not go home?" she asked.

I took her hand, having kissed her, and led her to a couch.

"You will be obedient, Caroline?"

She nodded. Her eyes were faintly blurred with happiness, her cheek was velvety warm to mine. I felt for her breasts. The resilient mounds were snowy white and firm, the nipples like tiny cherries. In two years perhaps I would have her wed. It was not an experience I proposed myself to indulge in again. In the meantime I would nurture and develop her to a point where her usefulness would be unbounded.

"Wait for me in my room," I told her.

"You will not be long, Beatrice?" Her eyes were the spaniel eyes of Father, brushing my skirts, nudging my calves—reaching to caress.

"Of course not," I smiled. My voice was at its most gracious. I reached the caging room in but moments and there gazed for a moment at the tableau which still presented itself. Amanda breathed softly—sniffling a little at my entry. With quick efficiency I released him from her. His cock emerged bubbling at the tip. The very suction of her bottom had produced an energetic pulsing of sperm, it seemed. Amanda was as quickly released. As coyly as she endeavoured to hide her face from him, she could not escape the darting of her eyes towards the now almost pendant penis that had entered and injected her.

"Dress and go down, Amanda. Prepare yourself for departure," I said simply. With only her dress to don, she was ready in a moment, her face a dull pink as she passed him in the act of restoring his trousers.

"And Amanda . . ." I called after her.

She turned at the door, endeavouring with little sucess to bring a look of remoteness to her features.

"You will not disobey. I shall visit to ascertain your progress," I told her. A mischief seized me. I knew the butterfly thoughts in her mind—the bumbling and buzzing of words that escaped before she could speak them. "Your allowance will be increased. Is that not so?" I turned and challenged him. It would not be my way with others, but these—as I have said—were mere oddments of people.

"What?" he ejaculated. The coldness of my stare was evident. Ludicrous in its peeping as he strove to cover himself, his penis lolled palely through the unfastened gap in his trousers. A wan bird that had flown and returned. "Ah . . . ah, yes. . . ." he stammered.

I nodded to Amanda whose expression was a picture. Whether I had undone or encouraged her conversation I knew not. The door closed upon her with the silence of one who leaves an unread note behind.

"My aunt would have a bracelet. I doubt not that you will fashion one well," I told him.

"Ah, yes." He seemed for the moment incapable of any other words. In slightly dishevelled state he was led without. On the landing I paused, closing the door to the caging room with such solemnity as I felt was due.

"You will have her, of course, tonight," I said, "and in

the same mode. She is not however to be tied. The arm of a sofa will suffice. As to strappings . . ."

"Yes?" His lips quavered wetly. I found the sight not to my taste.

"Once weekly of a morning, immediately upon her waking. You will modify her with some pretty nightgowns —of a transparent variety, of course. Shell-pink and a pale blue would suit her. You will take her bottom formally and without preliminary caresses or kisses. It is desired," I said regally, knowing him sufficiently insensitive not to appreciate that I was bubbling with silent laughter within. Cosseted more than she had been before, and no doubt later to be endowed with her own small carriage, Amanda would lend herself to it, I thought, with less difficulty than he anticipated. Within days she would derive more pleasure from it than she knew.

He nodded as if we were engaged upon some solemn discourse of State. Our footsteps sounded quietly upon the stairs. Amanda waited patiently in the hall, her features slightly constrained. To her surprise I kissed her cheek. Outside the horses of his carriage pawed the ground impatiently, their heads tossing.

"The requirements are understood," I said to her.

Not knowing of what I spoke she nodded, bit her lip, stared briefly at him and then dropped her eyes. He, believing obviously that she and I had already discussed such matters as I had conveyed to him, took her arm with rather more of a beseeching gesture than he had anticipated.

I opened the door. It is never my intention to have servants present at such moments. Bowing, he allowed me to precede them. I moved towards the carriage, motioning to the hastily clambering coachman not to descend. I opened the door.

"Raise your dress to the tops of your thighs when you are

seated, Amanda, and so keep it until the end of your journey," I said. She blushed fiercely. Her eyes fenced briefly with my own and then indicated their surrender. "He will not caress you," I added as they entered, "you are both to remain constrained. Forward, coachman!"

Straining in their harness, the four horses moved forward. My last glimpse for the nonce of Amanda was of her thighs flashing, her lips parted in a rosebud O of wonder.

A ripple of laughter escaped me. My fingers toyed about the full, rich blooms of the rhododendron bushes which lined the driveway as I returned to the house. They had obeyed me—they would obey, no doubt for months, until a greater loosing of lust took them.

It was of no matter, though out of an impudence of power I would visit upon them later. The older female of the house—she who had sat so complacent upon our visit there—might then need attending to. I would anticipate no objections either from her spouse or from Amanda. The occasion would provide a first exercise for Maria.

NINETEEN

CAROLINE lay waiting for me upon my bed with a look of such tremulousness that I slid down upon her. The petals of her lips grew softer under mine.

"Do you remember French-drinking?" I asked her. She blushed, nodded and murmured softly, drawing me more protectively upon her. I toyed with her thighs gently and with my other hand ran my forefinger along the succulent curve of her lower lip. "You liked it?" I asked. She hesitated, then lisped a sibilant yes. Her breath flooded warm over my cheek.

"When we return I will dress you as a little girl," I said.

She giggled and clutched me tighter. "Will you?" she asked shyly. Her heart palpitated, our breasts bulbing together.

"There shall be sweetness, punishments and pleasures, Caroline. I shall bring you to them all. Fetch wine now—an uncorked bottle—go!"

So astonished was she at my sudden command that she leapt up immediately as I rolled away from her. "And a napkin," I added. Clattering with unseemly haste she was gone and had returned within several minutes. In the meantime I had stripped to my boots and stockings and told her to do the same. Then, before her wide-eyed look, I lay back with the napkin beneath my bottom and my legs spread and dangling over the edge of the bed.

"This is the way we shall French-drink in future," I told her and motioned for the wine, at the same time making her kneel between my legs. The bottle came cool, between my breasts. I inverted it so that the neck pointed downwards towards my belly, laid flat. The ball of my thumb held tightly over the neck.

Raising my feet I laid them against her back, impelling her mouth inwards where the lips of my quim awaited her first salute. Ah! the sweet brushing of her mouth, half shy, half bold. Slowly I eased my thumb from the bottle neck until it but covered half. The wine trickled down. Down in its trickling down it meandered. Over my belly coursing, into the bush of curls seeking.

"Lick—drink," I whispered. The cool flowing of the wine which I released in bubbling streams was sweet to my skin, yet no sweeter than the more eager lapping now of Caroline's tongue. The tip curled and filtered between the lips of my lovepot, seeking upwards to my sprouting bud as the wine rolled gaily upon it and was received into her mouth.

I longed to buck, but I dared not or the wine would have shivered in sprinkling sparklings everywhere. My legs quivered and straightened, sliding down from her back.

Brazenly I parted them wider, arching my toes as a myriad delicious sensations overtook me. The gurgling of Caroline's throat as she received the increasing flood of wine was itself music, yet I must not forget my place, my purpose, nor my disciplines.

"You shall French-drink so, Caroline—the prick in your bottom," I husked. "Wriggle your bottom as if now you were receiving it—lick faster!" I desired to cry out that I was coming, yet some instinct told me not to divulge even to Caroline the degrees of my pleasure. Muted whimpers broke from my pursed lips as a thousand tiny rockets seemed to soar and explode in my belly. The saltness of my spillings in their spurtings no doubt communicated itself to her in a fine spray over her tongue.

I sighed, relaxed, and knew at long last my pleasure. My thumb covered the mouth of the bottle anew. I permitted no more to flow. With a tender but firm motion I pressed her mouth away. I was truly soaked.

"Bathe me," I murmured. I rose and preceded her into the bathroom. "Do not speak—you may speak later," I told her. The sponge laved me. I arose and was dried again. I took her then to the basin, bending her over it with my hand gripping the nape of her neck and washed her face.

We returned to the bedroom where I lay back full length. A scent of saffron came from the drawer of my dressing table where Mary or Maria had evidently sprinkled it with herbs. Waiting with owl-like eyes of blue, Caroline sat tentatively beside me and gazed down upon me. My fingers played with the backs of hers.

"Do you understand?" I asked.

Her lips moved as if to seek words that had long flown.

My arm reached upwards, looping about her neck and drawing her down of a sudden so that the corner of her mouth came to mine.

"You will know your purities, Caroline. The O is a purity. It circles within and without itself, knowing no otherness. Your mouth is an O—your bottom presents an equal roundness. Between your thighs the O has surrendered itself in its outerness to an oval, an ellipse. Within its knowing is the O—between your bottom cheeks another. The O of your roseness. The male stamen will enter it and impel the long jets of its succulence within. You will receive, absorb—even as your mouth absorbed. Did it not?"

I seized her golden hair, making her squeal. Her face lifted in startlement. Then, by a loosing of my clutch, she slithered down and buried her nose between my breasts. Her arms encircled my waist.

"Do not punish me for it," she murmured.

I played with her locks, running my fingers through the silky curls.

"Punishments and pleasures, Caroline. Have I not told you? You will suck it in my presence, bent upon your task. The while that it throbs in your mouth your bottom will receive the whip."

"Oh, please no! Beatrice, no!"

"There shall be stables, too, Caroline. I have engaged Maria to keep them clean—to monitor my captives. Shall you be one?"

Caroline dared not to raise her eyes. Her mouth nuzzled between the orbing of my breasts. I waited long on her reply. The whisperings of shyness, shyness in her mind breathed their illicit thoughts upon me.

"Shall . . . shall it be as with Frederick?" her whisper came to me aloud.

"Penis-bearers?" I mocked her lightly. "I shall have you blindfolded sometimes, my sweet. You will not know who your stallion is."

"Will you not love me, Beatrice?"

I drew her up slowly until her face came over mine. Broadening my stockinged thighs, I allowed her legs to slip between mine and pecked at her lips.

"In obedience there is love—in love there is obedience," I said. I slid my hand upwards beneath the long fall of her hair at the back and took her neck between thumb and fingers. It pleased me to do so even as I sensed that it pleased her to be held in this way. I felt her trembling. The moist lips of her pussy nestled into my own.

"Have you not been stilled, Caroline?"

"Please kiss me—please, I want your tongue," she husked. I smiled. Her moods were as the light passing of summer clouds. I could reach up and touch them.

"Suck upon it," I breathed. Possessed as I am of a long tongue I inserted stiffly into her mouth. The suction of her lips was delicious. She moved them back and forth over the sleek, velvety wetness and murmured incoherently while I squirmed my hand down between our bellies and cupped her plump little mount. The curls frizzed to my fingers. Caroline squirmed, endeavouring to bring her button to my caresses, but I laughed within her mouth and smacked her bottom suddenly with my free hand making her yelp.

"D . . . don't!" she bubbled. Her face hid itself against my neck. "What is stilled, Beatrice?"

"The male stem in your bottom, my love—urging, gliding, deep in. There it stays for a long moment and is withdrawn."

"OH!" I could feel the heat of her blushing against my skin, "it . . . it would be too big!" she stammered.

I laughed. The ceiling received the pleasure in my eyes. A warmness flowed over me. Caroline had, after all, been reserved for the cock I would present to her.

"Your bottom cheeks are deliciously elastic, Caroline. The first time you will experience considerable tightness, but you will yield. You will feel the veins, the knob, the inpushing—the breath will explode from your lungs. But on the second," I went on, ignoring her wrigglings that were meant together with her silly, tumbling words to express refusal, "on the second bout, my sweet, your rosehole will receive the repeated pistoning of the cock until you have drawn forth his spurting juice."

"No! I don't want to!" she whined.

"Then you will be whipped first—or strapped perhaps."

With each word then I smacked her bottom loudly, ringing my free arm tightly about her slender waist while she jolted and struggled madly. Finally I let her roll free. Her pert bottom was a perfect picture of pinkness, splurged with the paler marks my fingers had imprinted. Drawing up her knees she sobbed and lay with her face against the wall.

I waited. After a moment when she had not moved I rose and put on my dress. Immediately she spun over and lay upon her back.

"Wh . . . what are you doing?" she asked. Her eyes were blurred with tears, her hair mussed. In such disarray she looked at her prettiest.

"Maria will learn to use the strap on you now," I said severely. Without looking at her I brushed my hair in the mirror.

Caroline rolled immediately off the bed and, kneeling, hugged my legs.

"If I say that I will—please!" she begged.

I glanced down at her and then resumed my brushing. "It is not for you to say, Caroline," I answered briefly. I moved away from her by force so that she slumped upon the floor, looking as forlorn as she could contrive. It was a game that she was learning, I could sense, yet her knowing must not be too great. Not as yet. In a year or two perhaps. The fine balance of yes and no was truly here.

I looked down upon her once more. The violin curves of her hips were indeed sweet, the upsweep of her bottom infinitely appealing. With a slightly greater plumpness than Amanda there possessed, Caroline would surrender eventually to her pleasures more than she knew.

Head hanging and eyes clouded, she rose slowly to her feet and endeavoured to hug me. I stood unmoving.

"Do not let Maria strap me hard," she murmured. Her fingertips fluttered about my back like petals falling. When I did not answer she snuggled into me closer, manoeuvring one thigh and trying to press it between my own. "Do you not love me?" she whispered.

I raised her face at last.

"In all my being," I replied softly and kissed her mouth. "Now go upstairs—I shall strap you myself. You will learn."

"Yes," Caroline whispered. It was a plea rather than acceptance. Another moment and I might have relented.

"Go," I said again, "wait for me—over the bar. Leave your dress here."

Her footsteps slouched. Her look was a lostness—sweet and well contrived. It passed across my mirror and was ignored.

Five minutes later the strap swathed heat across her cheeks.

In her sobbing cries as she gripped the bar beneath was her surrender.

TWENTY

IN the week that followed I made ready for our departure. Katherine made her future appointments with me. Maria's husband, Ned, was interviewed formally. He would come into service with me, I told him carefully. His uniform would be that of a valet. He would be put to many different tasks. Maria—I was pleased to think—had evidently scolded him into agreement beforehand since his continued nodding during my conversation became almost tiresome. His physique, however, was entirely suitable—his thighs good, his loins muscular.

There would be Frederick also, as I apprised Katherine. He had been permitted no further licence with her. To ensure that, I had kept him to the house while she was elsewhere.

The day before leaving I called her to my room.

"You will devise a play—not too simple a one, Katherine. I will have it performed a few weeks after we have settled in again."

She curtsied playfully. I had not asked her to sit. "Shall there be many players? Six or eight, perhaps?" she asked.

I merely nodded as if my thoughts were already elsewhere. It is a simple enough trick. It keeps those I need, desire—or would work to my will—in a state of slight imbalance.

"You will engage Amanda in it," I said. "We shall then best see her progress—and her silver stocking bands, no doubt. And the maid at Arabella's house—the young one who attended upon us. I want her. You will obtain and bring her."

The play itself would be of no great importance. The words, the acts, could be peeled away at my discretion and replaced by others. Arabella possessed a controllable wantonness, as I had witnessed. She would present a voluptuous example to occasional novices. As to the young maid who had lain at my feet after tonguing me—the sly-eyed, sloe-eyed one—there was a hint of impudence in her eyes that I could quell at will or use according to my whims.

On the morning of our departure I made Caroline ready in the prettiest of blue dresses with matching bonnet and patterned stockings of the same shade. For myself I wore a modish back dress, severely buttoned to the neck, with a pearl choker. My bonnet was a three-cornered one. It gave me a slightly swashbuckling air without looking flirtatious. As to the kid gloves I had desired, I had now a dozen pairs in different shades. My uncle's wallet had been well pillaged.

Maria and Jenny, I attired in oatmeal cloaks with hoods. Beneath, they were naked save for stockings and boots. I placed them, together with the clothes and cases my uncle had been made to endow, in the smaller of two carriages outside.

Aunt Maude had relinquished Maria not without reluctance. We had discussed much in private. I broadened her horizons. There would be garden parties from Friday to Monday on half a dozen occasions throughout the summer, I said. We did not use the word "weekend." It was considered common. From the gatherings, both my aunt and myself would make a discreet choice among the females and, occasionally, their escorts—whether related to them or not. They would be drawn aside and would receive special attention. The likeliest females would be cosseted and flattered. In the privacy of bedrooms there would be means of bringing them to undress and even of displaying them to the males through peepholes in adjoining rooms.

"The males will be discovered at their peeping by one or other of us," I told my aunt. "It will be necessary for them of course to be punished. Their fear of betraying the conventions will make them submit. The females they have viewed and who will remain naked—while being aroused by Maria or Jenny or another—will then be shown to the peepholes in turn and may gaze upon the males in their bondage."

Such discourses pleased my aunt immensely. My imagination flourished. Even so I kept some secrets to myself. There were caves I would not allow her to enter. She sensed that. It gave her a certain air of diffidence as I flourished my images before her. There were moments when she seemed to stand in awe of me.

We stood in my room prior to descending to where Caroline and my uncle waited. Amusement and apprehension mingled in her eyes as I pressed her to the wall and bid her stand with her arms at her sides. I took her cheeks in my hands. They were as smooth as a girl's.

"You enjoyed?" I asked. She knew well enough to what I referred. Her smile was cautious but impish.

"When your bottom took his cock? You were superb," she breathed.

I kept my eyes level with hers. As one enraptured by a fine statue I ran my little finger delicately along her lower lip.

"You will be used," I said.

"With Frederick?" The question was a little unexpected but I absorbed it without expression. She had veiled her desires carefully.

"Yes—and with others. You will obey me, Maude."

It was the first time I had used her Christian name. "Yes," she acquiesced softly. The tips of our tongues touched as if with a timidity at our own daring. My sails were hoisted, set. There would be no turning back for her. Our tongues in their moistness moved. So slowly they moved as if Time had been run down.

"And your uncle?" she asked. Our breaths flowed together. He had not been put to servicing since he had mounted me. His eyes had grown haggard in his waiting. I had had him placed in a small separate bedroom from my aunt. I licked her tongue for the last time and stilled the hands which would have reached for my bottom.

"You may keep him in a stiff but agonised state, his receptacles full. In a few weeks time he will be put to servicing the first of my novices—until then he is not to be milked," I said. My eyes held a strain of severity as I spoke. I released her gently. It would amuse her to follow my instructions, I knew.

I swept down before she could speak, thus forcing her to follow me. In the hall my uncle's glance was timourous. I afforded him a kiss on the cheek. In turning away from him my gloved hand made passing contact with his penis which stood proud in his breeches. The caress would appease him for the moment.

The sun stood high above us as the door opened, flooding the vista with golden light. "The sun is God," the great painter Turner had said on his deathbed twenty years before. It had shone upon his bed, they had said, in the very moment of his uttering the words and dying. In that moment I believed him. Caroline moved in her beauty beside me. Her skirts swept the ground. I went as I had come, yet in my going I was one reborn. Passing the rhododendron bushes I caressed their leaves and blooms once more.

The silence of plants pleases me. They see without seeing, watch without watching. Subservient to the touch, they yet never surrender. Crush them and they will reappear next year or elsewhere. Their chemistry compounds miracles. They are there in their thereness. At night they sleep yet they know not Time. They breathe softly yet are not heard.

"I would be as a plant," I said to Caroline. In the carriage I held her hand. The figures of my aunt and uncle standing on the steps diminished.

"Yes, I would like to be a flower," she replied. She had not understood. It did not matter. Her voice was simple and childish. I saw her as she would be—rooted to the stamen, the pale fusing of the cock with her bottom. She would rock, moan and whimper in her beginnings. Later I would teach her silence. She would know the silence of the plants—the impelling flood of the sap in her gripping. Rising up the embedded stem, it would flood her in its submission. With its last throbbings it would withdraw. She would know the victory—the power.

The house waited for us, bereft of servants. My aunt had

dismissed them. It was a wiseness. Only the older gardener, Perkins, was left. He was too withered for my purposes. Appearing at the approach of our carriages, he doffed his hat and acted as footman in opening the door. I gave him the most gracious of my smiles.

The rooms at least had been aired. From the kitchen came smells of butter, cheese and herbs. Mingled withall was the scent of bread which had been left that morning. Milk waited in stone jars, covered with fine net. In the stone-walled larder, lettuces shone their fine diamonds of cool water. All was well. My letter to Father floated upon the oceans. Maria and Jenny removed their cloaks and moved about us. Curiously nervous as they appeared of the windows and the gardener's eyes, I had them don dresses. The proprieties had to be observed. With the drawing of the curtains at night, our world would be enclosed.

"Shall there be visitors?" Caroline asked. Maria made tea. We took it in the drawing room.

"Many. There will be masquerades, amusements, entertainments, Caroline—garden parties. You will enjoy those."

I would chain the girls to trees at night, I thought. Chinese lanterns would float and sway among the leaves. I would move among them with a feather, their dresses raised. One by one they would be carried in for pleasuring. The stables would be candlelit.

Did Caroline read my thoughts? Laying down her cup she rose and looked beyond the French windows to the lawn where the silver larches swayed in their slender beings.

"You will not love me as the others—I know it," she said sullenly. "Will all the girls be young?"

"No." I rose in turn and moved to her. My hand rested upon her shoulder. Her head lay back. Her fine hair tickled my nose. "Some will be matrons—firm of body. The summerhouse is large within, is it not?"

Caroline nodded. I could not see her eyes. "Yes—why?"

"We shall furnish it to our tastes. What is within?"

"A divan—no more." Her bottom in its roundness moved its globe against my belly. "Father said . . ." she began. I stopped her.

"I shall ordain. There shall be ottomans, rugs, silken cushions, shaded lamps, a small scattering of whips and birches to tease your bottom. We shall have our privacies there—our secrets, our voluptuousness. Do you understand?"

"Yes," she husked. She turned and nestled in my arms. "Will you . . . will you make me do it there? No one will see, will they?"

"No one—no one but I. You will offer your bottom as you gave your mouth."

So saying, I raised her dress at the back and fondled the satiny orb. Feeling between the cheeks I circled the ball of my thumb about her rosehole, making her clutch my neck and quiver.

"It will b . . . b . . . be too big!" she quavered.

"Be still!" I said sternly, "hold your legs straight, reach up on your toes. Hold so, Caroline!"

"Blub!" she choked. Easing my thumb within I felt her warm tightness to the knuckle, her gripping. Her gripping was as a baby's mouth. With a smooth movement of my free arm I scooped her dress up at the front and cupped her nest. It pulsed in its pulsing. My thumb purred between the lips and parted them.

"Still!" I commanded her. "Hold your dress up—waist high, Caroline!" She obeyed, swaying on her toes as she was. Her eyes glazed as I moved my thumb up deeper into her most secret recess, toying with the small perky button of

her clitoris at the same time. Unable to keep her balance, her heels chattered on the floor.

"Wh . . . Wh . . . Whoooooo!" she whimpered.

I allowed her the sounds, the small outburstings of breath. The warmth emanating from between her silky thighs was delicious. Had I not intended now to keep her separated from the others I would have had Maria or Jenny enter and tongue her.

"Be quiet now—be quiet now, darling," I coaxed. I had moved to her side in the moving of my hands. Her fingers sought to release her uplifted skirt and clutch at air, but by some silent command they stayed. The folds drooped but a little. The pallor of her thighs gleamed above the blue darkness of her stocking.

The natural elasticity of her bottom eased a little until I was able to insert my thumb fully, my fingers flirting with the nether cheeks. The oiliness of her slit increased—its pulsing fluttered.

"B . . . B . . . Beatrice!" she stammered. Her head hung back until I almost feared she might collapse. An intense quivering ran through her. The curving of her straightened legs was exquisite. Of a sudden then her head snapped back, her shoulders slumping as I withdrew my thumb.

"OH!" she choked and would have slid to the floor had I not caught her. "Oh, B . . . Beatrice!"

"So, it shall be," I smiled and kissed her mouth. She would make much of it in the beginning. In time she would kneel for it with glowing pride—an altar of love. After two years, as I had promised myself, she would return to her everydayness, free to leave or to stay.

You ask why—and I know not. Who shall be free and who not? I had chosen to ordain. There were those who would follow and those who would not. Through the dark glass of unknowing they would seek my image. At night they would huddle in the woods, the shrubs, among the wet leaves—crying for my presence. I would untie their childhoods. The last drums of their youth would beat for them. In their submission would be their comforting. Wailing and crying they would succumb to that which they had longed for. The whip would burnish their bottoms in their weepings. The velvet curtains would be drawn—receive their tears. The dry leaves of the aspidistras would accept their lamentations. In the mornings they would be as choir girls, clothed in white. Calmed from the storm they would talk softly, twittering. I would absolve their sins. I would teach. In time they would learn the inferiority of men—the penis-bearers, the money bringers.

For as such only would men be used. I would teach.

Now we composed ourselves again. Caroline sat fidgeting a little while Maria removed the tray. She would prepare a meal for Frederick and her husband on their arrival later, I told her. Together with herself and Jenny they would eat in the kitchen.

Maria bobbed and nodded in her going. She saw herself perhaps as the head of a small conclave of servants, but I would know how to split and divide.

"Caroline, you will have a maid shortly," I said when the door had closed. She looked at me in astonishment. We had lived in comparative modesty before. "I?" she asked.

I smiled and seated myself beside her, rolling her warm and slender fingers in my hand.

"A young servant who at present serves Arabella and her family," I explained. The idea had come sudden upon me. It would serve to elevate Caroline above the others.

"She shall be unto you as a handmaid. You will train her," I said. "She will attend upon no one else other than at my bidding."

"Train her?" Caroline's face was a picture. "Oh! shall I be as you, then?" she asked naïvely, but I forebore to laugh. Her sweetness was apparent. She would lend herself with the seeming innocence of an angel to all that I intended.

"In time perhaps, Caroline. You have been stabled, at least. And cupboarded. Was that not splendid? Did you not enjoy it?"

She nodded, her cheeks suffused. "No one will ever tie us together again," she said.

"But I may tie you together with your maid," I laughed. The shyness in her eyes darted with the delicacy of moths. "She is pretty—a perfect body. Pleasures and punishments —did I not tell you?"

"May I . . . may I strap her? Just sometimes?"

The question was as unexpected as Aunt Maude's had been about Frederick. Deep pleasures were in my being at such questions. I had the power to answer or not—to assuage, persuade, refuse, mollify or conquer.

"You wish to? Who else did you wish to strap?"

A knowingly attractive pouting of Caroline's mouth offered itself to me.

"Amanda. She wanted silver stocking bands—did you know?"

"Yes, I knew. What else did she say?"

Caroline's eyes retreated. They appeared to take an immense interest in my corsage. "She . . . she said if they were silver, solid silver, she would let him."

I breathed lightly, betraying no surprise. Ah, Amanda! the depths of you! But no doubt she had seen no other escape and so sought to make her excuses. Caroline had obviously probed and asked. We know not those we know when they are away from us. Father would lie with women in their bronzeness. He would swish their bottoms with a fly-switch. Langourous they would lie, the sweat between their nether cheeks, up-bulbing, offering—the delicate twitching of flesh as the switch descended. Servants would come and go, bearing tea, blind in their unseeing.

"You may strap her, yes, but only playfully," I said, recalling Caroline's question. I would draw her into my plans a little, yet leave her always on a fringe of wondering —the last lines left undrawn, a mid-air hesitation. Workmen would come shortly to commence the building of the stables, I told her. I had promises that the work would be completed in two weeks. The main bedroom which Father normally inhabited would become now my own. Caroline would take the room next to it. The stables would have an annexe that would form a caging room.

My plans expanded with every breath—her face a mirror to my thoughts. Withal a question poised itself on her lips as a bird alights and rests upon a sill.

"But when Father returns?" she asked.

My face was a blankness. "And naturally we shall furnish the summerhouse last," I said as if there had been no pause in my words. Clearly she was about to speak again when the doorbell sounded. Jenny hurried to answer. In a moment she returned bearing a *carte de visite* on a tray. I took it and read. The name meant nothing to me: THE REV. HORACE AMES.

"He seeks but a moment and is accompanied," Jenny said. I did not ask by whom. Such questions tend to indicate some unsettlement of the mind. I waved my hand languidly for her to admit them. Caroline adjusted herself, fanning out her skirt. Her composure at such times pleases me.

In a moment the door opened to admit a gentleman of not unpleasing aspect in his middle years. He was alone. He sought my indulgence, he said. His dark suit and clerical collar gave him a slightly hawkish air. They had travelled from Kent, he explained, to inspect a neighbouring house he intended to purchase in the parish. Alas, the hub of one of the wheels of their carriage had collapsed and the house agent had not arrived with the keys, as promised. They had waited an hour in the gardens. Now with the lateness of the day he sought to find momentary shelter for his daughters.

"They are waiting beyond?" I asked.

"In the hall, Madame. I thought not to disturb you overmuch. . . ."

"Oh, but you must bring them in!" I interrupted swiftly. "My sister will see to it. Will you not have a sherry? Of course we shall afford you all that you need. What a hopelessness you must have felt in your waiting."

Overwhelmed by my reception as he appeared to be, he took the proferred glass and sat as the door reopened to admit two young ladies of apparent exceeding shyness. Both were prettily dressed and bonneted, but their boots had a sad and dusty air of those who have travelled far.

In seconds they were introduced. The taller, Clarissa, was it seemed eighteen. Jane was her junior by three years, but already with sufficient nubility to attract my eyes. Both were brunettes with retroussé noses and pleasing mouths. Their ankles were slender, though mainly hid.

"How were you to return and when?" I asked. I affected a great bubbling, flooding him with words while Caroline attended to the girls with refreshing drinks. By some fortune, Frederick and Ned made their appearance during my discourse. I summoned the latter immediately to the wheelwright who I knew sometimes put carriages out on hire. Within the hour the fellow returned bearing the solemn news that only a small phaeton was available with scarce room for three for a longish journey.

In the meantime, however, I had gathered much. The Reverend Ames was to replace the present incumbent vicar.

Yet, it seemed, he had business that very night in Gravesend, where he must return.

"Then the girls must stay," I proclaimed immediately while both sat darting the most timid yet enquiring glances at me. No doubt like he they wondered at my Mistress-ship of the house in my relative youth.

"Nay—it would be a terrible imposition, Madame. In particular since I shall be unable to return for a week. Is there no hotel or hostelry close?"

"Where they would stay unchaperoned?" I asked. The thought soon mended such objections as he had tendered with obvious civility, hopeful as he had obviously been that I would take them in. They were after all of our own class. The conventions were being observed. The additional presence of Caroline placed a perfect seal upon the matter.

At five-thirty, having partaken with us of a cold collation which Maria had prepared, he was ready to depart. His daughters sat demure as ever, the dutiful kiss imprinted on their cheeks with his parting. Crowned as I was with his gratitude, I saw him to the driveway where the phaeton waited.

Clarissa and Jane would be well seen to, I assured him. His hand received my own and held it rather warmly. He was a widower, I had learned.

"They will be in the best of care—of that I am now certain," he proclaimed and kissed my hand gravely before ensconcing himself on a rather hard seat.

"The very best," I assured him, "they will be seen to in all respects."

"A week, then," he said and waved his hand. He seemed rather enamoured of my gaze, I thought, as his carriage trundled forward. I watched it to the gates. The door lay wide still—invitingly open for me. Its panes of coloured glass fragmented glittering streaks of light along the wall of the hall where the sun struck. The light brushed my cheek as if in benediction as I walked through and entered the drawing room.

Caroline had engaged herself more animatedly, it seemed, in conversation with the girls. Perhaps in her knowing, she thought as I. I clapped my hands and smiled, expressing my pleasure at their presence.

"First we will bathe you and refresh you," I said. They had removed their bonnets. Their hair flowed long and prettily about their shoulders. I reached down and took the hand of Jane. "Come—I will see to you first. Then Caroline may attend upon Clarissa," I said.

A light flush entered Clarissa's cheeks. "Oh, but . . ." she began. I stopped her with a further smile.

"I know," I said softly. I induced infinite understanding in my voice. "Normally you bathe alone, but in a strange house—and the taps are really so difficult. . . ."

I allowed my voice to trail off vaguely in leading Jane out. She had the perfect air of a Cupid, I thought—an impression that increased as I first ran the water and then undressed her. Her form was exquisite, her breasts the firmest of pomegranates on which the buds of her nipples perked as if beseeching kisses. Her bottom had a chubbiness that my hands sought slyly to fondle in removing her drawers. In stepping out of them she betrayed with many a blush the pouting of her cunnylips which nestled in a sweet little bush of curls.

Tempted as I was to finger them I urged her into the water where she sat with the warm scented water lapping just beneath her breasts. "I shall soap you—may I?" I asked. Seemingly not wishful to escape the admiration in my eyes she sat mute, pink-cheeked, as I passed my soaped hands first over her deliciously firm breasts. Plump and silk-smooth as they were, her nipples erected quickly, her lips parting to show pearly teeth as I playfully nipped the nearest between two fingers.

"How pretty you look," I breathed, "may I kiss you?"

In speaking I passed my free hand up the sleekness of her back, cradling my palm beneath her hair. Hot-flushed as she was, her lips came peachlike to mine with sufficient parting for me to intrude my tongue. For a long moment her own coiled back, but then came timidly to meet mine. My hand passed over the succulent weight of her other breast. Its nipple burned like a thorn to my palm. Her lips moved farther apart in her wondering, but I intended not to spoil her yet. I assumed an air of loving fun and joviality that would disperse itself as a balm to her conscience.

"It will be fun, Jane, will it not?" I asked and received a shy, lisped yes. For the rest I soaped her carefully, fondling every crevice and hillock I could reach without making my further gestures too obvious. The drying took longer—particularly in the gentle, urging motions of my towelled hand between her thighs. Her flush rose considerably then, her knees bending as she clung to me.

I said no more, donating but a light kiss to her mouth before putting her into a robe. In a week I would work wonders with her. And night had yet to fall.

Hearing the opening of the bathroom door from below, Caroline brought Clarissa up. The water lay warm still. It was the custom then for two people to use the same bath, the water supplies being often uncertain.

Clarissa's eyes grazed mine in their coming. I knew her eyes. I would neither fondle nor kiss her in the bath. While Caroline escorted Jane to her room, I led Clarissa within and waited as one waits while she disrobed. In chemise and stockings her figure was similar to Amanda's save that her bottom was larger. Nervously fingering the straps of her chemise, she waited evidently for me to leave.

Instead of doing so I gathered up the clothes she had discarded. I did so as by reproof. Then with a pettish gesture she removed her last garment and stood in her stockings. Her mount was plump, her thighs elegant, feet small. Her breasts, though not large, were of perfect roundness.

"Call me when you have bathed and I will bring you a robe—or the servant shall," I told her.

The relief in her eyes was evident. A smile of assent meandered to her lips. Removing her stockings and stepping daintily into the clouded water, she sat down.

I went out, leaving the door ajar and placing her clothes where she would not find them. Jane would be easy. I knew her kind. Loving, warm and submissive, she would absorb the cock with wriggling wonder. A week was almost too much. With Clarissa it would be different. I had allowed her but one small victory, and her last. The surprise of the strap would come all the more clearly and stingingly to her that night. Maria would hold her.

I moved in my musings beyond, into the lumber room from whence the ladder led to the attic. A sadness of dust was upon the rungs. Beneath me, the water in the bathroom splashed as it would splash upon the prow on the tall ship in its sailing.

And its returning . . . its returning . . . its returning. . . .

More Erotic Fiction from Headline:

EROS IN TOWN

Anonymous

When the aristocratic Sir Franklin Franklyn and his half-brother Andy arrive in London to claim their inheritance, they find not the respectable family home they expected but the most lascivious of brothels. Frank takes things into his own hands and transforms the town-house into the most luxurious, romantic house of pleasure in all London. Here, every desire is catered for, any amorous wish met.

Not to be outdone, Frank's saucy sister Sophie declares that women are as much slaves to desire as men, and to prove her point she establishes a stable of lusty lovers patronised by the most elegant ladies in the land.

Thus both brother and sister indulge themselves in an orgy of sensuality that surpasses even the wildest flights of erotic fantasy . . .

Also available from Headline – EROS IN THE COUNTRY – the first volume in the sensual adventures of a lady and gentleman of leisure.

FICTION/EROTICA 0 7472 3199 0 £2.99

More Erotic Fiction from Headline:

A LADY OF QUALITY

A romance of lust

A N O N Y M O U S

Even on the boat to France, Madeleine experiences a taste of the pleasures that await her in the city of Paris. Seduced first by Mona, the luscious Italian opera singer, and then, more conventionally, by the ship's gallant British captain, Madeleine is more sure than ever of her ambition to become a lady of pleasure.

Once in Paris, Madeleine revels in a feast of forbidden delights, each course sweeter than the last. Fires are kindled in her blood by the attentions of worldly Frenchmen as, burning with passion, she embarks on a journey of erotic discovery . . .

Don't miss VENUS IN PARIS also from Headline

FICTION/EROTICA 0 7472 3184 2 £2.99

More Erotic Fiction from Headline:

Sweet Fanny

The erotic education of a Regency maid

Faye Rossignol

'From the time I was sixteen until the age of thirty-two I "spread the gentlemen's relish" as the saying goes. In short, I was a Lady of Pleasure.'

Fanny, now the Comtesse de C---, looks back on a lifetime of pleasure, of experiment in the myriad Arts of Love. In letters to her granddaughter and namesake, she recounts the erotic education of a young girl at the hands of a mysterious Comte – whose philosophy of life carries hedonism to voluptuous extremes – and his partners in every kind of sin. There is little the young Fanny does not experience – and relate in exquisite detail to the recipient of her remarkably revealing memoirs.

Coming soon from Headline
SWEET FANNY'S DIARIES

FICTION/EROTICA 0 7472 3275 X £2.99